Brookside 2
Weathering The Sto

KATHLEEN POTTER

Brookside 2

Weathering The Storm

A Methuen Paperback

A Methuen Paperback

WEATHERING THE STORM

First published in Great Britain 1986
by Methuen London Ltd
11 New Fetter Lane, London EC4P 4EE
Copyright © in television format and novel Phil Redmond Enterprises Ltd 1986

British Library Cataloguing in Publication Data

Potter, Kathleen
  Weathering the storm.——(Brookside; 2)
  ——(A Channel Four Book)
  I. Title   II. Series
  823'.914[F]   PR6066.07/

  ISBN 0-413-41430-2

Printed and bound in Great Britain
by Richard Clay (The Chaucer Press) Ltd,
Bungay, Suffolk

Chapter One

Karen Grant sat in Abercrombie Square in Liverpool. Around her, in the late spring sunshine, fellow students went about their business. She was happy. This time last year she'd still been at school and now here she was at the university, enjoying her course and her involvement with student journalism. And, best of all, planning to move into a flat with Guy.

When she'd told her mother.

Guy couldn't understand her anxiety about that. 'She likes you, you know that. She won't mind. Everybody does it these days.'

'Not where me mam comes from.'

'I'll tell her if you don't want to.'

'No. Leave it to me. I'll let it slip out gradually that we're . . . you know.'

Guy smiled. 'I know . . . more than just good friends?'

'Yes.'

Karen knew he thought her scruples were old-fashioned. It hadn't been as easy as she'd thought to throw off the morality of her Catholic upbringing. But although he didn't understand he didn't mock her for it. She loved him for that.

Guy went across the square for the evening paper.

'Here we are. Flats galore. We're bound to find something.'

'Yes, but will it be something we can afford on your grant? I won't get anything, with living in Liverpool.'

'We'll manage. With a bit of help from my dad. He'll sub us if I twist his arm.'

'Are you sure?' said Karen. Her family had thought they'd really gone up in the world making the move from the council estate to Brookside Close, but since she'd been at university she'd discovered a whole new world. She still hadn't got used to the easy belief of Guy and people like him that somebody – an aunt or parent – would always send a cheque for an emergency, or some new clothes, or a holiday, or even sometimes for nothing at all.

She liked sharing in the benefits but sometimes her conscience stirred. So many of her fellow students came from a comfortable, middle-class background like Guy's. How could they know what life was like for people who had no such security behind them and no future but the dole? In this city there were two different worlds and Karen had a foot in both.

'Let's find somewhere more peaceful,' said Guy, and she followed him across the grass. Suddenly she stopped, clutching his arm.

'No. Not that way. Look. Over there.' And over there, luckily too preoccupied to have seen Karen, was Matty Nolan. Uncle Matty to the Grant kids, their parents' oldest friend. What had stopped Karen was what was preoccupying him. He was lying in the grass, indecently close to a woman.

'What's the matter?' asked Guy.

'It's Matty,' said Karen.

'So?'

'That woman he's with. She's not his wife.'

Across the square, Matty leaned over Mo Francis and couldn't believe his luck. Two years he'd been out of work, no chance of another job, useless, thinking his life was over. And now here he was, feeling young again and planning a fresh start with this exciting woman.

Karen had never seen Mo before but she had a good idea who she was.

'My mum was right,' said Karen. 'There is something going on.'

'It certainly looks like it. Unless they're auditioning for the lead in a romantic movie.'

'It's not funny. The one he's with, she must be Mo Francis. He met her at the class, the Return to Learn.'

'How d'you know?'

'Me mam told me. She goes, too, and she said they were keen on each other. She's been upset about it. Teresa – Matty's wife – is her best friend.'

'I can see why she's upset.'

'I'll have to tell her I've seen them.'

'Don't.' Guy was definite.

'Why not? I can't just leave it.'

'What can your mum do if she knows?'

'I dunno. Speak to Matty maybe.'

'I wouldn't tell her if I were you. Just pretend you haven't noticed. Interfering never does any good.'

Karen looked at Matty again. He was poking a finger between the buttons of Mo's blouse and whispering in her ear. Poor Teresa. No way could Karen not tell her mother.

At home in Brookside Close, Heather Haversham was getting ready for a very important meeting. She dressed for it carefully and with uncharacteristic uncertainty, changing her outfit twice before she settled on something that seemed just right. It mattered that things should go well.

She picked up a bottle of perfume and sprayed herself lavishly. As she finished, it spluttered and failed. It had been expensive perfume, a gift from Tom. For a moment she looked at the bottle, remembering what might have been if she had married Tom. Then, firmly, she threw it away. That was in the past: there was no going back. Today was very much about the future.

In the kitchen, she laid the table for five. Nick and herself at each end, Ruth and Adam one side, Scott the other. She hesitated, wondering whether to put Adam next to her or next to his father. Adam, Nick's youngest, ten years old, cricket-mad and a real charmer. Not least of his charms was that he'd taken to Heather right from the first meeting. Today was the first time she would meet the others.

On reflection, Heather decided to put Ruth next to her. It wasn't enough to get on with Adam; she was going to have to get on with all the children. After all she'd be seeing a lot of them when she was their step-mother.

Heather smiled at the thought. She was hardly the stereotype of a step-mother. She was too young for a start, not that much older then Ruth. Perhaps it would be better to think of herself as an older sister. Heather had always wanted a sister. She was looking forward to the evening very much.

She was putting a bowl of flowers in the middle of the table when the phone rang. It was Nick.

'Hello.' Just the sound of his voice made her feel happy.

'What are you ringing for? I thought you'd be on your way.'

'Adam's playing cricket for the cubs. It's half term.'

'I know. He told me.'

'I've said I'll pick him up. The others are coming from Barbara's on their own. I won't be long.'

Heather went back to her table and adjusted a fork. She hoped Nick wouldn't be long. She'd come to rely a great deal on his warm good nature and his calm good sense. She thought of him at the cricket match smiling proudly at Adam and felt a great pang of longing.

Outside in the Close she heard voices. Through the window she saw the two young people. The boy, just growing into a teenager, that must be Scott. And the girl, older, flirting with Rod Corkhill. That certainly was Ruth. Heather took a deep breath and went out to meet them.

Ruth scowled when Heather passed on Nick's message.

'He should have been here,' she said. 'Or told us to come later.'

8

'I suppose he forgot,' said Heather.

'As usual.'

Heather was taken aback by Ruth's sharpness. It was true that Nick was forgetful, but it wasn't something Heather minded very much. Indeed she found it a refreshing change after Tom's attempts to organize her life. Still, it wasn't up to Heather to defend Nick to his own daughter. 'I'm sure he'll be here soon,' she said.

He was ten minutes, and it was a long ten minutes. Heather had struggled with a conversation in which Scott had said virtually nothing and Ruth had done no more than necessary to be polite. Heather was beginning to realize how very little she knew about present-day teenagers. Most of her friends, as Nick had once said, were accountants, accountants and more accountants. The children were as relieved to see Nick as she was.

'Where's Adam?' asked Ruth.

'Match not over. I got the time wrong. I said I'd go back.'

'So long as you don't forget,' said Ruth. Almost as if she were the parent and Nick the child.

'Don't fuss,' said Nick. 'There's time yet. We don't want to spoil his bowling average, do we?'

With their father there, the children thawed, and Heather began to feel better about the evening. Better enough eventually to let the big news slip out.

'We've got plans. We're going to get married.'

Adam Black was sorry his dad couldn't wait to see him bowl out the tail enders. Still, he'd get on with the job. He ran up, fingers curled round the ball as Paul Collins had showed him, and hurled his missile.

'How's that . . .!'

Another small boy looked at his spread-eagled wicket and trailed off the field.

Adam was on form that day. And besides, the opposing team were a pretty poor lot. By six o'clock they were all out; that match was over.

After the congratulations, Adam washed and changed. He trailed across the grass to the gate of the sports ground and watched and waved as his friends were driven away. More than once he was offered a lift but he was afraid to miss his dad so he refused. Besides, it'd be a bit complicated to explain where he was going. Since his mother had gone to live with another woman, he'd found out that other people's mothers were inclined to be nosy, especially about his home situation. It was difficult enough to explain the relationship between his mother and Ginny. He didn't at all relish any questions about who Heather was.

But once everyone else had gone, Adam began to feel very bored. He was longing to see Heather. He'd liked her ever since they'd first met. He knew the way, he was pretty sure, and if he kept a look out for his dad's car . . .

Adam set off along the road.

Annabelle Collins put the phone down, scarcely able to hide her delight.

'Guess who that was, Paul?'

'Sarah Hutchinson?'

'How . . .'

'Did I guess? Not difficult with her voice. I don't know why she bothers to use the telephone.'

Annabelle sighed. Paul had certainly taken a dislike to Sarah. And what she had to tell him wasn't going to help.

'She rang up about you becoming a magistrate.'

'Oh yes? And no doubt I'm too old for that, too.' Since his early retirement after an American takeover at his old firm, Paul had been finding it difficult to find things to do.

'I'm afraid so.' Annabelle was genuinely sorry when she saw Paul's disappointment. It did seem very wrong that someone with his skills and experience should be considered of no use. He might be over sixty but he still had a lot to offer.

'Oh well, I never thought it was the thing for me

anyway,' Paul said. Annabelle wasn't deceived by his stiff upper lip; it didn't make it any easier to pass on the rest of Sarah's message.

'They've made further enquiries. They want to put *my* name forward. It seems I'd be an ideal candidate.'

'Interfering woman.' Paul meant Sarah Hutchinson.

'She is. But still, it is a public duty. If I was asked I don't see how I could refuse, do you?'

And Paul couldn't.

His mood didn't improve as they set off for a meal out. Annabelle offered him the keys to her car.

'Would you like to drive?'

'Certainly not. Far too many cars on the roads these days.' Since he'd lost his company car Paul had become rather tedious in extolling the dangers of driving. Annabelle noticed however that he didn't mind being a passenger in hers when it suited him.

They were discussing wedding presents for Heather and Nick, when the car in front of them stopped so suddenly that Annabelle only just avoided going into the back of it. Paul was out of the car in a flash. 'Drivers!' said Paul. 'See what I mean? I'll give him a piece of my mind.'

'Don't make a scene . . .' But Annabelle's words faded as she saw Paul's shocked face. When she joined him she understood.

He was staring down at young Adam Black spread-eagled in the road.

Nick was setting out the champagne he and Heather had bought for a celebration when Paul drove back up the Close. He parked in the middle of the road and ran for Heather's door. Nick, hearing the squeal of brakes, went to meet him. Paul's face was ashen. 'It's Adam,' he said, 'An accident. Come at once.'

Nick patted his pockets frantically. 'Where are my car keys?'

'Get in with me,' said Paul. 'I know where to go.'

After they'd gone Heather and the children stood in stunned silence. Ruth was the first to break it. 'What if . . .' She couldn't go on. Suddenly she seemed like a little girl. Despite her own fear Heather tried to comfort her. 'We just have to wait. I'm sure it'll be all right . . .' Ruth turned on her, her hostility plain to see. 'It's all your fault,' she said. 'If we hadn't been coming here none of this would have happened.'

By the time Paul came back with the news that Adam was not badly hurt, it was too late to heal the breach. Heather had offered to run Ruth and Scott up to the hospital to meet their mother. Ruth's rejection was cruel. 'What would you do there?' she said. 'It's nothing to do with you, is it? After all, it's not as if you're family.'

When they'd gone, walking purposefully down the Close, not looking back, Heather started to clear the festive table. She looked at the five places she had set. She had hoped for so much. A ready-made family had seemed exciting. She'd imagined days out together, meals with talk and laughter. A family without ties which would have interrupted her career. She had so hoped that the older children would be like Adam, open and trusting, ready to like her. And then this.

She put her head down on her pretty tablecloth and cried.

Next door, Doreen Corkhill carried a mug of tea out to Billy. Now that he'd recovered from the first shock of losing his job he was making himself useful, building a garage with knock-off bricks from his brother Jimmy. They'd come home one day to find them piled on the drive when Jimmy had needed to get rid of them in a hurry.

Doe admired the way Billy put his back into the job: she admired his back too as she watched him barrowing sand to lay the foundations. They hadn't had an easy start, her and Billy, with having to get married, and they certainly hadn't had it easy since. But it was a good marriage, and she still fancied him even after all these years.

Tracy Corkhill looked through the bedroom window at her parents. They looked settled for a bit. One of the problems for Tracy now that her father was on the dole was that he was round the house all the time. She had no chance to get the phone.

Tracy dialled, and listened for a minute to see who was on the line. This telephone Chatline had been a godsend to her these last few weeks. Without it she'd have been very lonely indeed. After her affair with her teacher, Peter Montague, she'd had to change schools and her old friends weren't allowed to see her any more. She had no chance to make any new ones with her mother keeping an eye on every move she made.

'Any girls on the line?' an unknown male voice said.

'I am.'

'What are you called?'

'What d'you do?' That was a different voice.

'I'm a model.' And Tracy was off into her fantasy world in which she was grown-up and free and not just a schoolkid whose parents didn't understand. . . .

Through the window Tracy saw her mother get up and come towards the house. She put the phone down quickly. But not quick enough.

'Who was that?' asked Doreen.

'Me nan.' But as soon as she saw her mother's face Tracy knew she'd got it wrong.

'Your nan's in Southport. Who was it?'

Tracy knew she was no match for her mam. Or her dad. When Doreen brought him in to confront his daughter he was horrified.

'You done what?' he said. 'You little fool. D'you know the size of our phone bill? Two hundred quid.'

'Why?' asked Doreen. 'Whatever made you do such a thing?'

Tracy tried to explain about the loneliness. Standing in the playground on her own, pointed at. What she didn't say was how much she still missed Peter. That was something she'd always have to keep to herself.

'That's it, then,' said Billy, when Tracy had gone up-stairs. 'It explains the phone bill. What it doesn't explain is how we're supposed to find the money to pay it.'

Doreen had her usual answer. 'Credit card. It's what they're for isn't it, to help out when you're a bit pushed.'

'Doesn't pay it for you though, does it? They send bills too.'

'It's just for now,' said Doreen. 'We'll pay it off easy when you get a job.'

If, thought Billy. And how much will there be to pay off by then? But that bit he kept to himself. What could Doe do? And how would two of them worrying help?

Sheila wished that Bobby would worry more. It seemed as if he was deliberately ignoring what was happening to Matty, what Sheila had seen with her own eyes. Every time she mentioned it and tried to get him to intervene, he just talked about the strike at Bragg's Engineering.

It didn't make Sheila feel any better when Karen told her what she'd seen in Abercrombie Square. This was real evidence and it was no good running away from it.

'Tell your dad,' said Sheila. 'Perhaps he'll take a bit more notice of you.' But all Bobby would say was what he always said. 'It'll pass over, Shei. Just keep out of it. It never does any good poking into other people's lives.'

Only this wasn't other people. It was Matty. Matty and Teresa – they went together like Bobby and Sheila, always had done since they were kids. Now, Teresa was living in a fool's paradise, looking after her kids, making the giro cheque last, wearing herself out with her job as a school cleaner, doing her best, whilst all the time Matty was playing around with Mo Francis. Sheila felt awful not telling her, not giving her a chance to fight for her marriage. But then again, what if Bobby was right? Supposing she told and it made it worse, made Matty leave? So in the end Sheila said nothing. But she didn't stop worrying.

For Terry Sullivan, life was on an up. He was getting on

very well with Vicki Cleary, very well indeed, since the trouble with her brother's van hire firm had been sorted out. Vicki was the right girl for him: outgoing, easy to know, willing to take a chance on things. She bucked him up, he calmed her down; they suited each other. She was spending more and more time in Brookside Close and that suited Terry fine.

But as Terry went up, Pat went down. His relationship with Sandra, which had begun as they comforted each other as they were held hostage in their own home a year before, was coming apart at the seams. The cause was perfectly clear, at least as far as Pat was concerned. His name was Tony Hurrell.

He was a young doctor Sandra had met at the hospital where she was a sister in the private ward. They'd really got to know each other at the bedside of a patient, a young woman of Sandra's age, who'd had a hysterectomy. Her grief at not being able to have any more children had really got to Sandra, and to Tony too. Tony had questioned the consultant's policy about such operations.

'Somebody should look into it. Half the operations he does are quite unnecessary.'

'He's a good doctor,' Sandra had said.

'Maybe he is, but he's only human. These are private operations, remember. The money goes in his pocket. Don't tell me he doesn't think of that when his daughter's getting married or he wants a new car.'

Sandra, persuaded, had joined Tony Hurrell in a search through the hospital records to see what they could find out about Mr Cribbs-Baker's operating record. This couldn't be done in work hours, as Sandra explained to Pat. She had to stay late.

Pat thought she was making a big mistake, and didn't hesitate to say so. Especially when he came home one day to find Tony Hurrell ensconced in his lounge with a pile of medical records.

'You gone mad?' he asked Sandra. 'That's way 'gainst the rules. You're risking your job for this.'

After that, Sandra didn't bring any more work home. She spent longer at the hospital instead. Looking through the records, she steadfastly maintained every time Pat challenged her. Pat's problem was that he didn't believe her. He'd seen the way Hurrell looked at her, and the way she looked back. Thinking of them together, his guts churned with jealousy. Where was she? What was she doing? Was he going to lose her?

The fact that business with the van hire was no more than moderate didn't help. It didn't seem to bother Terry. Terry was content so long as he could afford the occasional bevvy, play footy and see Vicki. Pat wanted more. Needed more if he was to have a chance of competing with a real-life hospital doctor.

It all came to a head one night when Pat had had a particularly hard day. Sandra had phoned in sick and taken the day off work, but when Pat came in with some magazines and flowers she was up and about, bright as a button, and in the middle of an animated phone call to Dr Hurrell. Her face, and the sound of his rival's name, were like a red rag to a bull for Pat. He flung the presents at her and shouted, 'Aren't you supposed to be ill? Or is that just an excuse for when you want to say no in bed?'

'I'm better, that's all. People get better, don't they?'

'You can when you want to phone him. But not when I want you to talk to me. But then I'm not a doctor, am I? And it's him you fancy, not me.'

'For goodness sake, will you listen? I don't fancy him.'

'If it's not him then, who is it?'

'Nobody. I don't fancy anybody.'

'Well, you make it clear enough you don't fancy me.'

'Of course I still fancy you.'

'Prove it.'

'Not when you're in this kind of a mood.'

After that there was nowhere to go but down. In the end Sandra collected a spare duvet and carried it into Kate's bedroom.

Kate's bedroom. They still called it that. Even a year later. Because it hadn't been used since that awful day a year ago when Kate had died there, shot by poor John Clarke. Poor John Clarke. Sandra never imagined she'd think of him like that. And yet it was true that he'd been more pathetic than dangerous; the shooting had really been a tragic accident. Kate had died unnecessarily, trying to stop Clarke shooting himself.

In this room, this very room. This bed. Lying there, remembering, there was no way Sandra could fall asleep. She remembered, too, the nights after the siege when she and Pat, the two survivors, had been too afraid to spend more than seconds apart from each other. The nights in particular had only been bearable as long as she had the comfort of Pat's body. At midnight Sandra gave up. She got up and walked across the landing. Quietly she opened the door of Pat's – her – bedroom. Pat wasn't sleeping either.

'Sand?'

'Don't say anything. Just hold me.'

Gratefully, Sandra climbed back into bed.

Paul Collins woke every morning to repeated images of young Adam, sprawled in the road, caught by the car's wheels. Would he ever forget it? Certainly he'd never forget the feelings of dread and despair as they'd waited for Adam to open his eyes. He'd met Adam just at the right moment, when the novelty of being redundant – he and Annabelle had decided to call it early retirement – had begun to wear off, and he realized he had an awful lot of time to fill. Adam's enthusiasm had reminded Paul that the world was full of possibilities. The moment when he'd thought such enthusiasm, such possibilities, might never be realized would stay with Paul. He was determined to do what he could to make sure it didn't happen again, to Adam or any other child. He'd write letters to the paper, he thought, and get in touch with some councillors he knew. But it didn't work out quite as he'd expected.

Kathleen Monaghan came marching up the Close one sunny afternoon and found Paul in the front garden. He'd got in touch with her after he'd seen a letter she'd written about road safety. He thought he might enrol her in his campaign. Kathleen didn't see it quite like that.

She started off on the attack. ''Course, you would have a car.'

'Why not? A lot of people have.'

'Especially them that live in the suburbs.'

'What's wrong with living in a suburb?' said Annabelle. She'd already decided she didn't like Mrs Monaghan.

Kathleen Monaghan didn't care whether Annabelle liked her or not. 'D'you know what it's like to live on an estate?' she said.

'No.' Thank goodness, thought Annabelle, but she kept that bit to herself.

'Well then, you won't know what it's like to live in fear for your child's life every time you hear a car roaring up the street.'

'What's that to do with Paul having a car?'

'Goes to work in it, does he?'

'Yes. Well . . . he did.'

'Those drivers that roar past our houses, the ones that think they're Niki Lauda, they don't live on the estate, do they? They're just using it as a racetrack on the way from their posh offices in town to their posh houses out here. Along roads built for car owners. Trouble is, most of those that live there can't afford cars.'

Paul decided it was time he intervened. 'About Adam,' he said. 'I believe his isn't the first accident on that bit of road.'

'No. It's a blackspot.'

'Then something should be done.'

'We've been blocking the road. You thinking of joining us?'

Paul took care not to catch Annabelle's eye. 'I was thinking more of a petition . . .'

'A petition!' Kathleen was scornful. 'How long will that take? How many more kids'll get killed?'

'Killed?'

Kathleen Monaghan looked directly at Annabelle. 'Killed. It happens, Mrs Collins. My son didn't get away as lightly as Adam Black.'

Chapter Two

Sheila had agreed to have the Return to Learn tutorial group at her house. Normally she didn't mind that: it saved a journey and was a lot more comfortable than the Education Centre. But now things were different. By having Mo in her house, offering her tea, wasn't she betraying Teresa? And as luck would have it, Matty and Mo were the first to arrive. Sheila greeted them stiffly, ignoring their attempts to be treated as a couple, and had the satisfaction of seeing Matty's unease when she pointedly asked after Teresa. What she didn't know was that they were now having more than a clandestine affair; last night Matty had told Teresa he was leaving her and had moved in to live with Mo.

When the class got going Sheila began to feel a bit better. She always enjoyed the classes, especially when the group discussed things. It'd never been like this at school, but then the teachers had been different: more concerned with keeping order than making things interesting. Alun Jones, the group tutor, wasn't like that. He didn't tell you things exactly, but he showed you how to find out. With his help Sheila was discovering a brain she'd never known she had. She'd begun to take a real interest in the history of Liverpool. She had realized that history wasn't just about dead people, it was about how what happened in the past affected what was going on now. 'It's not your fault there's no work here,' she'd explained to Damon one day when he was feeling down. 'Just that trade's moved south now we don't get stuff from America.' It wouldn't help him get a job but maybe it could stop him blaming himself for being out of work.

The time passed quickly as it always did. Halfway through, Alun suggested they had a break and Sheila went through into the kitchen to make a cup of tea. Sally Dinsdale followed her.

'Can I have a word, Sheila?'

'Of course, love.'

But Sheila's heart sank. She knew what it would be about. It wasn't the first time Sally had leaned on her and she didn't suppose it'd be the last. Sally's husband was a wife-beater.

Sheila had learned a lot since she'd started on this course. One was that things weren't always what they seemed. Sally wasn't like someone off the estate; she was nicely spoken and well dressed, and she lived in a posh area. Definitely what Sheila's mother would have called respectable. And they weren't that short of money; Sally's husband had a regular job. If Sheila hadn't seen the bruises with her own eyes she would never have believed it.

'He had another go at me last night.'

'You poor thing.' Sheila had given up advising Sally to leave: all Sally would say was that Ken was nice when he was in a good mood. That wouldn't have been good enough for Sheila, not after some of the injuries she'd seen, but it seemed to be good enough for Sally. Perhaps the fact that Sally's father had been a wife-beater too had something to do with it. Sheila had learned that all she could do was offer sympathy.

There was a knock at the door as the kettle boiled. Sheila poked her head out of the kitchen. 'Can you see who it is, Alun? I'm just brewing.'

It was Teresa. Looking awful. She walked straight in and looked round. Sheila just stared at her, teapot in hand, not knowing what to say. Teresa seemed strangely calm. She looked round the room.

'Which one is it, Shei?' she said.

In moving to protect Mo, Matty gave the game away. Suddenly Teresa wasn't calm any more. Fists flying, she went for her rival.

'You whore,' she said. 'Selfish bitch. Out for what you can get. How about me, eh? What about his children?'

Mo moved back, hands up to protect her face. 'Leave me alone. You don't know what you're talking about. It's not like that. We love each other.'

'Love!' Teresa screamed the word. 'I'll give you love. You're destroying us. We're destroyed. . . .' She grabbed for Mo's hair.

It took two of them, Matty and Alun, to hold her off long enough to give Sally a chance to get Mo out of the house. Sheila just stood as if paralysed, hating herself. She should never have let it come to this. She should have done something. She should have made Bobby do something.

At last Teresa calmed down and crouched, sobbing, in the corner of the couch. All her rage was gone, she looked utterly defeated. Sheila went to put her arms round her. 'Oh, Teresa . . . I am sorry. . . .' But Teresa pushed her away.

'You knew, didn't you? You've watched them. You've had them in your house.'

Sheila couldn't deny it.

'What sort of friend is that? After all I've done for you . . .'

Those were the words that really struck home. All night they stayed with Sheila as she tossed about, not able to sleep. 'After all I've done for you . . .' Teresa had done so many things for Sheila. It was Teresa who'd made excuses to Sheila's first boyfriend when she'd dropped him for Bobby, Teresa who'd been the first to know when Barry was on the way, and the first, after Bobby, to see him. Many a time she'd wept on Teresa's shoulder over Barry's wildness. And then there was the awful time when she'd been so depressed after Claire was born. 'After all I've done for you . . .'

At any rate, thought Sheila, Bobby will have to take it seriously at last. Surely now he'll have a word with Matty.

But as so often these days, Bobby came home from his work as District Secretary of the ETWU with troubles of his own. He scarcely seemed to be listening when Sheila tried to tell him how awful it had been.

'It wasn't like Teresa at all. She looked like somebody gone mad, Bobby.'

'Perhaps you should go round and see her. Have a word.'

'It's not her that's in the wrong, is it. It's Matty who needs talking to. You're his mate, he'll listen to you.'

'I'll see what I can do.' Only Bobby knew there was nothing he could do. Matty was besotted with Mo, he'd said so himself. 'I love her, Bob. She's given me new hope. . . .' Nothing Bobby or anybody else said would change his mind. Bobby had promised Matty not to tell Sheila that and perhaps it was for the best. If she knew things were that serious it'd only worry her more.

In any case, most of Bobby's attention these days was somewhere else: at Bragg's Engineering. He was trying to figure out what exactly was going on.

It was six weeks now since Dave Butler had come into Bobby's office asking for help. He'd shown Bobby the pay slips, his own and that of one of the labourers to back up his case, and Bobby had agreed with him. What was happening wasn't right. Skilled men, men who'd served their time as apprentices, men who'd accepted low pay and been dogsbodies for years in order to learn a trade, were taking home less in their pay packets than a man on the brush.

It was the productivity deal that was doing it. The firm had agreed to pay a bonus on productivity above the norm. And they were doing well; with the number of firms that had gone down over the past few years they more or less had the field to themselves. So of course the employees were feeling the benefits in their pay packet. Except, that is, for ETWU members who had a separate agreement which excluded them from the bonus.

Bobby had gladly agreed when Dave had asked for help

23

in fighting the case. The difficulty lay higher up, with George Williams, the area secretary.

Bobby and George had been friends for years; it was thanks to George's encouragement that Bobby had got his job. Always up to now they had seen eye to eye. So what was going on?

George's advice to Bobby had been simple: keep out of it, keep things quiet; calm things down. But it was too late for that; the men had been on unofficial strike for three weeks now. Still George wouldn't ask the National Executive to make it official.

Dave came to see Bobby again. 'The lads are fed up. More than fed up, steaming mad.'

'I don't understand it,' said Bobby. 'You've got the support of the district committee haven't you?'

'That's right.'

'Then George should be taking it to national level with his full backing. What the hell is he playing at?'

'Personal politics, if you ask me,' said Dave.

Bobby was horribly afraid Dave might be right. He didn't like to think it but he had heard a rumour to that effect. But in keeping his nose clean George was being disloyal to his own men.

'You know what they say about us up here,' said Dave, 'Scousers . . . hot-headed militants. Easy enough for the National Executive, isn't it, safely away down there in the affluent south? Don't they realize that we're the front line? Are we supposed to say nothing whilst they throw us on the scrap heap?'

'If they don't, I do,' said Bobby. 'I'm with the lads all the way. You can tell them from me the strike's official.'

Any doubts Bobby might have had were dispelled by Dave's delighted face. 'That's great, Bob. Just telling the lads will raise their morale.' But after Dave had gone, Bobby was still puzzled. Where was George in all this? Would he back the strike? And if not . . . but that didn't bear thinking about. With time to think Bobby realized how far he'd exceeded his authority. Everything depended on George's backing.

He didn't get any backing from Sheila. She was upset when she heard what he'd done.

'You've made the strike official without the backing of the NEC? I can't believe you mean it.'

'Why? You ought to know I'd never sell out.'

'It's not worth taking a stand about. It's about differentials, not jobs. You know what I think about that.'

Bobby did. Sheila had already made her position plain. In her view unions should be fighting for true socialism, meaning equal pay for all, not differentials. Bobby didn't want to get into all that again.

'For weeks you've gone on about sticking by Teresa.'

'What's that got to do with it?'

'You didn't want to let her down, did you? Because she's a friend. I'm talking about loyalty, Shei.'

'You're putting our whole future at risk over this.'

Bobby was afraid of that, too, but he wasn't going to let on to Sheila.

'I'll get a chance to explain. The National Executive will understand. I'm the man on the spot, aren't I?'

'So's George Williams. And he's area secretary. Won't they wonder why he's not backing you?'

'He will.' Bobby's words sounded braver than he felt. 'And if not, I stand or fall on my record.'

'You fall? You mean all of us. Including the baby.'

'Oh Shei . . .'

'You already know what the NEC think of the branch. And you'll be tarred with the same brush.'

'I can't let the lads down. It's a matter of principle.'

'Try telling our Claire that when she needs new shoes.'

Rod Corkhill's eighteenth was a day to remember. Or to forget, as far as Doreen was concerned. He intended to celebrate in style and asked his parents if he could have a party.

Billy, increasingly worried about money, said no at first.

25

'Who's going to pay for it? D'you think we're made of money? And then there'll be a pressy as well.'

But Rod assured them he'd settle for a pair of socks if need be, and his friends'd all bring bottles, if only . . . And Doreen, to Billy's surprise, agreed.

'He's got to celebrate, Billy. He's coming of age.' She looked at her tall son with pride. It didn't seem a minute since, dizzy from the gas and air, not sure what had hit her but very proud, she'd first held him in her arms as a new baby. And now he was a man. Well, nearly. That was certainly something to celebrate. Besides, she wanted to show off her new house.

Billy was more realistic. The morning of the party he started to organize Rod and Tracy.

'Clear the living room . . . Furniture, ornaments, the lot. If it'll move, move it.' Doreen came back from the shops to find the house stripped.

'Ar, eh, Billy. What you doing?'

'What does it look like? Getting ready for the party.'

'D'you want them to think we've got nothing? I want all that stuff putting back.'

'I've worked for this all the hours God sends. I'm not having it ruined.'

'They're only having a party.'

'They're a gang of kids. And they're having ale. Remember your twenty-first.'

Doreen did remember. Beer over her mother's best dress, two broken windows and a ciggy setting fire to the curtains. 'You win,' she said. 'Clear the kitchen too.'

All Rod's friends came, and a lot of people he didn't know as well. Tracy had invited some of her friends but none of them turned up. She never really got to the bottom of why. 'Busy,' they said. Or 'Me mam wanted me to baby-sit.' Danny, a friend of Rod's from the old school, was more brutal. 'What d'you expect?' he said. 'I bet they weren't allowed. They wouldn't want to get a bad name now would they?'

'Why don't you go and pick your nose,' said Tracy,

26

pushing away the arm he was trying to slide round her.

'Only do it with teachers then, do you?' he said spite-fully.

Round them, in the Corkhills' denuded living room, lit only by disco lights, other girls danced and flirted and had a good time. Tracy, too proud to cry, went up to her room. She fixed a chair under the door handle. If she was going to be on her own she'd make sure she really was on her own, free at least from insults.

In the bar at the Swan Doreen drank her gin. And then another. 'Shouldn't we go back now, Billy? God knows what they're up to. We should have stopped.'

'You heard what the lad said. D'you want him to look a divvy? He's grown up, Doe. He can look after himself.'

'I only hope our Tracy's all right.'

'What's the point of living in a detached house?' said Paul.

'No,' said Annabelle, not listening. She was making out the bill for a buffet lunch.

'Are you listening?'

'Yes.' Annabelle added a few pounds on to her estimate for good luck. She had a tendency to forget that the catering business was meant to make money, and be rather over-generous with the cream or the garnishes.

'Well, can't you hear that racket from the Corkhills'?'

'Rod's eighteenth today.'

'Eighteenth or not, there's no excuse for this. D'you think his parents are there?'

'Bound to be. Doreen's quite a sensible woman. And very house-proud. She wouldn't go out and leave a house full of teenagers.'

'I'm going to have a word.'

When Paul knocked at number ten, a perfect stranger opened the door. A youth, oddly dressed, and in Paul's opinion distinctly drunk.

'Mr Corkhill?'

'Na.'

'Mrs Corkhill?'

'Na.'

'Well then . . .'

Rod pushed through the gathering throng. He, too, was none too sober but at least he knew who Paul was.

'Could you turn the noise down? Some of us are trying to get some peace.'

'It's a party.'

'You can have a party without deafening the whole Close.'

'You're only young once,' said another lout behind Rod's shoulder. 'Come on Corky, find us another can.'

'I've no other choice,' said Paul. 'I'll shall have to get the police.'

'Spoilsport.'

Upstairs in her room, Tracy huddled in bed. Even fully dressed and huddled in a duvet she couldn't stop shivering. She didn't get out when she heard the mocking voices calling after Paul, or when she heard the catcalls when the police came, or even when her mother, back at last, came to check up on her.

'Go away,' she said to an anxious Doreen. 'Just leave me alone. I'm all right. I'm tired. Can't you let me get me sleep?'

But she didn't sleep, not even when everything was finally quiet, and the Close was dark. She couldn't forget what Danny had jeered. 'Only do it with teachers do you?'

That was how other people said it. That she'd 'done it with a teacher'. As if Peter was any old teacher, instead of Peter whom she loved and missed and wanted to be with. She couldn't even talk about missing him, or about how much it hurt that he'd never replied to her letter. As if everybody thought that if it was never mentioned it'd go away. But it wouldn't go away. She was the girl who went with the teacher. The girl with a bad name. Would she ever live it down? She was fifteen years old and her mother watched every move she made and she had no

28

friends. Rod may have enjoyed his party but Tracy certainly did not.

The next day Rod woke up to find himself in bed with a permanent souvenir: a policeman's helmet. He fished it out from the bottom of the bed and memory came flooding back. Paul Collins complaining, and a policeman who Rod had recognized as a boy who'd left school the year before last. Tommo had accepted a couple of bevvys and enjoyed himself as much as anybody before he'd left with a token warning and without his helmet. Pretty cushy number as a job, he'd said. Good pay, good prospects and good fun. Rod liked the sound of that. Besides what else was there to do round here?

He broached the subject to his dad as they shifted furniture back that next morning.

'You know I'm leaving school this summer?'

'Well?'

'I thought I might join the force.'

'The force?'

'The police force.'

Billy was appalled. 'Are you still bevvied?'

'It's a good job.'

'Not for any lad of mine it's not.'

'Why not?'

'Your Uncle Jimmy, for a start. He's been fitted up more times than a tailor's dummy. D'you want to join the gang who's done it to him?'

'Let him do it,' said Doreen. 'D'you want him on the dole, like you? A few weeks and it's driving you round the twist.'

'Anything but a copper.'

'Oh yes? And who did you send for when our Tracy went missing?'

'That's different.'

'Is it?'

'Anyway,' said Rod, 'I'm eighteen now. Whatever you say, it's up to me.'

*

Two days after his accident Adam was out of hospital, in three back at school, and by the weekend back playing cricket. He recovered from the effects of that traumatic day quicker than Nick and Heather. Nick came round to see Heather the night of Rod's party, ready to make wedding plans. Heather was in no state to pay attention. One of the things she liked about Nick was his sensitivity to her moods but that made it difficult to pretend that she was feeling all right when she wasn't. When he asked her what the matter was she couldn't lie.

'It's Ruth.'

'What about Ruth?'

'I'll be her step-mother.'

'So?'

'She doesn't like me.'

'You've been reading too many fairy stories.'

'No, really.'

'It's just her way. She takes her time getting to know people.'

'It's not just that. She blamed me for Adam's accident.'

'How?'

'Because if you'd not been here it would never have happened.'

'If ifs and ands were pots and pans . . .'

Heather nearly hit him in her frustration. The other side to Nick's easy-going nature was an irritating tendency to bury his head in the sand.

'Don't you understand, she was looking for an excuse . . .'

'How can you say that? She's only a child.'

Heather heard warning bells. Ruth was Nick's daughter. Heather thought of her own father, who idolized her. This was tricky ground.

'I'm sorry. I didn't mean it like that. We were getting on fine. It was just unfortunate.'

'Yes. And Adam's right as rain now. Everything'll blow over.'

'I don't think it will.'

'It'll be all right, you'll see,' said Nick. Heather remembered Ruth's parting shot when she'd offered a lift to the hospital: 'What would you do there? It's not as if you're family is it?' She wasn't anything like as sure as Nick that everything would be all right. She had an uneasy feeling that Ruth didn't want her to be family. After her broken marriage to Roger and the end of her engagement to Tom Curzon, making a relationship with Nick had felt like sailing into a safe harbour after a rough passage. She didn't want any more adventures, any more upsets. She wanted to stay where she was, reassured by his certainty, resting in his calm, protected by the fact that he was older and wiser.

'You're right,' she said. 'It'll be all right.'

Paul had been invited to join Kathleen Monaghan's committee to try and get something done about the accident blackspot. It wasn't what he'd expected. What he'd had in mind was a one-man campaign of letter writing and lobbying and influence. He didn't mind if other people helped, but he certainly saw himself as the leader. Maybe he'd be interviewed on local radio or television, speaking on behalf of the inarticulate. But Kathleen Monaghan was not inarticulate; quite the reverse. Paul had difficulty getting a word in edgeways when she opened her mouth.

The committee's plan was to form a rota to block the road outside the sports ground in the school summer holidays. 'We'll hit 'em where it hurts,' said Kathleen. 'Stop their precious cars.'

But that was next month and in the meantime children were still crossing the road. Next month wasn't soon enough for Paul Collins, newly redundant and with time on his hands.

'What we need,' he told Annabelle, 'is a crossing patrol.'

'Is it legal?' she asked. 'I thought the council took responsibility for that kind of thing.'

'I suppose they do. But we can't wait for them. It'll take months to get through the system and meanwhile children are in danger.'

'You should be careful,' said Anna roguishly. 'It wouldn't look very good if I had my own husband up before me on my first day on the bench.'

'You don't know you'll be accepted yet. There's a careful vetting system you know.'

'I'm an ideal candidate. So Sarah said.'

Paul gritted his teeth and made no comment. He was fond of Anna, had to be after all these years and all the trouble over the children. But not when she was in one of her cat got at the cream moods.

Paul embarked on his campaign with the thoroughness he'd learnt in his years in the army.

First, a recce.

For two days he went, morning and afternoon, and watched the road. The most dangerous time was in the afternoon after school. Crowds of children with bats, balls, dogs, bicycles or just themselves made their way to the recreation ground.

Second, equipment.

Paul, at his own expense, bought wood, hardboard, and some tins of paint.

Annabelle, drawn by the smell of paint, came into the kitchen just as he was finishing.

'What is it?'

'What does it look like?' Cautiously Paul stood his handiwork upright. 'Be careful, the paint's still wet.'

'It's a lollipop.'

'Well spotted.'

'You can't just go and station yourself in the street with that thing. It's against the law.'

'What makes you think that?' For a moment Paul feared she might have an answer. For the past week, Annabelle had spent every spare minute reading, quite indiscriminately, the law books she got from the library. Debt, property, treason . . . what use would she have for treason in

Liverpool Magistrates' Court, Paul wondered? Luckily she hadn't covered road-crossing patrols.

'I don't know,' she said. 'I just expect it is. Besides, you're just going to look silly.'

'I'm not going to do it,' said Paul. 'I'm their organizer.'

Third, recruitment of staff.

Paul walked across the Close to talk to Harry Cross. Harry was, as so often, lovingly polishing his appalling orchid-pink car. The fact that he couldn't drive it didn't stop it being the pride and joy of his life.

'Hello. Nice morning,' said Paul.

'Won't last,' said Harry. He was not by nature an optimist.

'Nice to be out in the fresh air.'

'So long as you're well wrapped up.'

'Heard about young Adam, did you?' asked Paul.

'Knocked down, I believe.'

'That's right.'

'Kids these days. Never look where they're going.'

Paul decided on the direct approach. 'That's a very dangerous crossing. Something should be done.'

'You're right,' said Harry. 'The government should pull its socks up.'

'I don't think you can expect the government to concern itself with a crossing near Brookside sports ground.'

'Why not? We pay our taxes same as anybody else.'

'Self-help,' said Paul. 'I think it's up to us to do something. We could save lives.'

'I've got a kidney donor card,' said Ralph, who had joined them with a fresh bucket of water. 'Always carry it. See?' And he fished in his back trouser pocket to show Paul.

'That's no use till you're dead,' said Paul. 'I'm talking about doing something now. Crossing patrol. Near the sports ground.'

'Give us something to do I suppose,' said Harry.

'I'm on if you are,' said Ralph. 'Anything I can do to help, I will.'

Paul pulled a coin from his pocket. 'We'll toss this. Find out who goes first.'

'That's only two.'

'Yes . . .'

'What about you?' Ralph had pulled a box of matches from another of his pockets and was breaking two of them.

'Three matches. We each take one. Shortest first, longest last.'

Paul tried to protest but they were two against one. So, only six weeks after being a senior manager at Petrochem, Paul Collins was standing in the middle of Dortmund Way with a home-made 'Stop' sign.

Chapter Three

For a few days after his reconciliation with Sandra, Pat felt better. She slept curled up in his arms, clinging on to him. He wanted nothing so much as to look after her. He even began to hope that one day soon he might raise the subject of marriage again.

But as soon as Sandra felt better things went wrong. Twice she was late home from work, several times Pat came in and found her on the phone to Hurrell. True, every conversation he overheard was about some patient and her operation, but Pat wasn't a fool. He strongly suspected that more personal matters were talked about when he wasn't there to overhear.

Jealousy tied his stomach in knots. He had a sour taste in his mouth which took away his appetite. He couldn't sleep and spent hours staring into the dark, not daring to move for fear of disturbing Sandra.

One day, coming home in the van with Terry, he shared his fears. 'She fancies him. I'm sure of it. It's obvious isn't it? He's a doctor . . . What am I? Half a van hire firm.'

'Don't knock it,' said Terry. 'We're not doing so bad.'

'Doesn't compare with being a doctor.'

'Sandra's not a snob.'

'That's not all.'

'Oh?'

'She's . . . you know . . . not interested in me any more.'

'She's busy.'

'In bed I mean.'

'Oh, I see.'

35

The way Terry said it wasn't reassuring. They drove home in silence, each with his own thoughts. Terry remembered Michelle and the awful night he'd come home to find her in bed . . . in his bed . . . with Albert Duff. He remembered, too, the times she'd been late back from the dancing class and answered his questions with lies. How could he reassure Pat? Sandra didn't seem the kind of girl who'd two-time a fellow, but then Terry hadn't thought Michelle was either.

Pat's thoughts were no more cheerful. Sandra didn't any more fall asleep in his arms. If he tried to put them round her, she turned away and rolled towards the edge of the bed. As far away as possible. And as for anything more . . . he'd been rejected so often it didn't seem safe to try again. Pat didn't have much to be cheerful about.

At last Sandra and Tony Hurrell had something to show for their hard work. They had looked through hundreds of Mr Cribbs-Baker's records in cases where women had had hysterectomies. Patiently they had compared the diagnosis with the lab report after the operation. And they had found six cases where there was a clear alternative to the operation, and yet the operation had gone ahead. Still Pat wasn't persuaded.

'He probably did it because that's his style. You know as well as I do, that one doctor works one way and one another.'

'These were private operations, Pat. The man did it for money. They could have had chemo-therapy or laser beam treatment.'

'Can I explain it to you as a simple van driver?' said Pat.

'If you must.'

'You buy a house and the surveyor tells you there's dry rot.'

'So?'

'You get some estimates. One says only half that wood needs replacing, another says safer to get the whole lot done.'

36

'What's that to do with Cribbs-Baker? I'm talking about people, not wood.'

'It's a matter of opinion, isn't it? Your consultant may be operating more than most to be on the safe side.'

'How about the fact each operation means money in his pocket?'

'The man's a professional, for goodness sake. You've got to trust somebody.'

'How about you trusting me then? For a change,' said Sandra. And that was another sleepless night for Pat.

Paul was taking his duties as a crossing patrol man seriously. He made a list of days and times and agreed with Harry and Ralph who would do each duty. Annabelle called them the lollipop army. Paul was disappointed that she wasn't more supportive. She seemed to be more concerned with worrying about the effects it might have on her chances of becoming a magistrate than the lives of little children.

'They only want respectable members of society on the Bench you know.'

'You are respectable.'

'But will you be if you do this? I'm sure they vet the husbands as well.'

'I'm only doing my public duty.'

'And breaking the law.'

'You don't know that.'

'*Probably* breaking the law then,' said Annabelle.

Rather to Paul's surprise he discovered that he very much enjoyed the crossing patrol. It gave him a feeling of power to see the cars stop as he raised his lollipop. And it restored his sense of being of some use in the world when the children ran safely across the road.

He began to feel rather fond of some of them, especially the younger ones. He got to know one or two of them by name, and they got to know him. Some of them even said thank you as they passed him. The older ones were a different matter. Some of them were downright cheeky, calling him Mickey Mouse and running across the road just after he'd moved off it. But that didn't put Paul off. He only needed to think of Adam, and what might have happened, to give himself fresh heart.

One day however the arm of the law intervened. Paul had just shown three children across and returned to the pavement when a policeman came up and asked ponderously, 'That's not an official lollipop, is it sir?'

'No, it isn't. But this is a notorious accident blackspot. It's a scandal there isn't an official lollipop here.'

'I quite agree, sir. But wouldn't it be better to make representations through official channels?'

'I'm doing that, too. But that takes time. How many children will be killed in the meantime?'

'We can't all go about taking the law into our own hands, can we?'

'It's my lollipop you object to, is it?'

'It is, sir.'

'Presumably there's nothing to stop me as an individual taking children across the road?'

'I suppose there isn't.'

'Thank you for your advice,' said Paul. He put his lollipop down and stepped into the road. It was surprising how vulnerable he felt without it. He wasn't at all sure whether the motorists would see him, or take any notice of his upheld hand. Still, duty was duty. Paul stood his ground as the children ran across the road. As soon as PC Plod moved off he'd pick up his lollipop again.

Once safely back on the pavement he looked round for the policeman; nowhere in sight. Then he turned for his lollipop. He was just in time to see it being picked up by a bunch of the older children, his usual tormentors. 'Come back,' he shouted. 'That's mine.'

They stood just out of reach. 'Mickey Mouse wants his lollipop.'

'It's private property.'

'Want to have a lick do you?'

'Fetch it back at once.'

38

'Come and get it then.' And they stood tantalizingly out of reach. Paul gave up; if it came to a race Paul knew who'd win. He set off home with as much dignity as he could muster. Bother the police. They were keen enough on interfering where they weren't wanted. Where were they when they were needed?

Heather was happy. Not only was she getting married, she'd been promoted. Keith Tench, her immediate boss and *bête noire*, had moved on and she'd been given his job. She arrived home in a celebratory mood.

Nick had got to her house before her – he seemed to be able to leave work early most days – and came round from the back garden to meet her, spade in hand.

'You look happy.'

'Why not? I'm getting married in two weeks, aren't I?'

'Funny, so am I.'

'Perhaps we should make it a twosome.'

'Perhaps we should.'

'Dirty hands or not, come here for a kiss.'

'It's a pleasure.' As ever, Heather felt safe in Nick's arms. It was so nice to be looked after.

'What were you doing in the garden, anyway?'

'That's my secret.'

'My garden.'

'I thought I was going to live here too in two weeks.'

'Still, I'd like to know.'

'Tomorrow . . . It's a surprise.'

'Let me see . . .' But Nick, anticipating her plan, drew the back window curtains. 'You'll have to wait.'

After supper, cooked by Nick, they looked over the plans for the wedding. It was going to be a quiet do: that was what they both wanted. Just family at the ceremony, then a few more people at the house for a buffet lunch.

'You did notify the register office, didn't you?' said Heather. It seemed almost too obvious to ask.

There was an awful silence. Nick looked at her.

'Oh no! I knew there was something.'

Heather's stomach lurched. Nick was absent-minded, true enough, and normally she didn't mind. But this was important, very important, the most important thing they'd ever do together, indeed. Surely he couldn't really have forgotten.

'You wouldn't be joking?'

'I wish I was.' And she knew from his face that he wasn't.

Heather was near to tears. 'What are we going to do?'

'It's all right. I'll sort it out.'

'How?'

'I dunno.'

'Supposing we have to put the wedding off?' Heather wasn't superstitious, she didn't throw salt over her shoulder or avoid walking under ladders or read her stars in the paper. But a wedding was in some way symbolic. She needed everything to go smoothly this time. She so much wanted her and Nick to have a good start.

Nick could see she was upset. He put his arms round her. 'I'll sort it out. First thing in the morning.' He felt Heather's shoulders shake. He had to do something now. Inspiration struck. 'Better still, why don't we ask Annabelle?'

'How would Annabelle know? I don't suppose she's ever been near a register office. I'm sure she had a long white frock and half a dozen bridesmaids. And the caterers booked months in advance. Can you imagine Paul ever forgetting about a licence?'

'She knows about the law though, doesn't she? She's been reading law books nonstop ever since she thought she might get to be a magistrate.'

'Yes, nonstop.' Annabelle's keenness was quite a joke between Nick and Heather.

'So maybe she's read about how to get married. Worth a try?'

'Worth a try. Let's go.'

It wasn't perhaps the ideal moment to call in the Collins'. Paul had just come back from his unofficial crossing

40

patrol duty to find a policeman ensconced in his house. And what was worse, the same policeman who'd stopped him. Annabelle introduced him as PC Moonan, community policeman. Even when she'd gone on to explain that PC Moonan had come to follow up Paul's enquiry about the Homewatch scheme, Paul didn't feel much better. This chap hadn't been at all understanding about the crossing patrol; why should Paul entertain him as a guest in his own home? Paul glowered when Annabelle, anxious, as a potential Justice of the Peace, to make a good impression, offered PC Moonan another cup of coffee.

Heather broached the problem. 'Nicholas forgot to notify the register office of our intention to marry and now it's less than three weeks. What are we going to do?'

Anna tried to help. 'I'm sure it'll be all right.'

'But how?'

'Well . . . things work out, don't they?' said Annabelle vaguely. She was so flattered at being asked that she hadn't the slightest intention of admitting that she had no idea. It was PC Moonan who came to the rescue.

'It's not the only way of doing it,' he said.

'What?'

'You can get married by licence.'

'A special licence. I never thought of that,' said Nick.

'Not special, just ordinary. Special's what people call it but in fact it's just a licence.'

'How long does it take?'

'Twenty-four hours.'

'We've got two weeks.'

'That's all right then. No problem.'

Back at Heather's, she and Nick celebrated with some more of the champagne. 'Plain sailing then.'

'Here's to us.'

'D'you think Annabelle was hinting?'

'About what?'

'When we were talking about the arrangements for the wedding after we'd sorted things out. When she was asking about what sort of reception we were planning.'

'She's had an invitation already. Why should she hint?'

'I mean about who is doing the catering. Do you think we should have asked her?'

'Oh no. Busman's holiday.'

'What?'

'I know, from living in a hotel. You can't be a guest and see to the food as well.'

'I suppose you're right. The Collins aren't coming to the register office though, are they?'

'No. I thought just my dad and the children.'

'And Joyce and Charles for witnesses.'

'I've never met Charles.'

'I've met Joyce.' Joyce was a fellow accountant and Heather's friend from Hamilton Devereux.

'I know you have. Don't change the subject. When do I get to meet him?'

'At the wedding.'

'Funny to have a witness I've never met.'

'Well . . . he's busy.' And Heather had to be content with that.

She realized she'd be quite glad when the wedding was over. They could be such tricky things; people so easily had hurt feelings or lost tempers. She'd already trodden well and truly on Harry Cross' toes by not inviting him. And she still wasn't at all sure if Ruth could be counted on to behave decently.

But all her worries faded the next day when Nick took her into the garden to look at his wedding present, installed with the help of Terry and Pat. The back garden was transformed. Instead of the wilderness it had been, there was a smooth turfed lawn, a few fledgling shrubs and, best of all, a sundial.

'It's lovely,' she said.

'A gift for my bride. Come and look what the sundial says. It's two hundred years old . . . and I think it must have been a wedding present then too. I had to look a long way for one with words like this.'

42

Heather stood happily holding Nick's hand as he read what it said:

> Hail bounteous sun that dost inspire,
> Mirth and youth and warm desire.

'Is that what it'll do for us?' she said.
'That's the general idea.'
'I can't wait.'

Try as she might, Sheila couldn't get Teresa's words out of her head.

'Call yourself a friend? When all the time you knew that Matty was carrying on with her? Now he's left me . . .'

The memory of Teresa's face wouldn't go away either. Screwed up with rage and pain, shouting obscenities at Matty, at Mo, at Sheila, even at Alun when he'd tried to hold her back.

'It's all your fault,' she'd yelled at Sheila. 'You didn't think about me did you? You knew all about it but you didn't think to tell me.'

Sheila knew that wasn't true, but she was haunted by the words and by Teresa's pain and fear. Teresa had been her friend since they were kids. They'd been girls together, young mothers together. Teresa had helped her come to terms with the shock when she'd found herself pregnant at forty-four and, until this week, had been such a help minding the baby, Claire.

Claire had cried at the new baby-minders, wanting Teresa, and Sheila had almost wished she too was young enough to be allowed to howl. God only knows what would have happened to Sheila's own marriage after Bobby's vasectomy if Teresa hadn't helped her see sense. Somehow Sheila had to help Teresa and Matty weather this crisis in their own marriage. Somehow she had to make Matty give up Mo. If Teresa and Matty split up who'd be safe? Besides, Sheila was still close enough to the traditional teachings of the church to fear for Matty's immortal soul. In the end Sheila could bear it no longer. She decided she must do something. As a first step she'd go and see Teresa.

Sheila walked along the familiar streets of the estate. They seemed to look shabbier than ever. Litter blew down the gutters in the wind that came up from the river, the paint on the corpy houses was peeling off and every blank surface was sprayed with names or slogans or expletives. She and Bobby had lived here for over twenty years before they'd managed to move to a house of their own. Had it been this shabby all those years? Had Barry and Karen and Damon looked scruffy and had running noses? Sheila was heartily glad to be living in Brookside Close. It wasn't something she'd give up easily. Things were going to be very different for Claire.

Sheila felt a pang of guilt. What right had she to feel like that? The people round here were the kind of people she'd been brought up with. People Teresa still lived with. Had moving made her into a snob, separated her from her roots? Perhaps it had. If so, how much more might education? Where might she end up if, as Alun wanted her to, she took the process of education further after the end of the Return to Learn course this summer? Alun wanted her to, Bobby didn't. . . . What did she want? For the first time in her life, Sheila, at the age of forty-five, wanted to do something for herself, something more than keep house for her husband and bring up her children. And she wanted it quite a lot. Enough, if need be, to risk Bobby's disapproval.

Sheila had decided to look for Teresa at work. What she had to say was best said out of hearing of Teresa's teenage children. She'd come at half past four when she knew Teresa would be at the school where she had her cleaning job, and yet, with any luck, the teachers and kids would be out of the way. Even so, Sheila's knees were shaking when she walked in through the school door.

In the main hall she stood for a minute, listening

44

carefully for sounds of someone at work: the clack of a bucket or the scrape of a chair. She didn't know what room Teresa was in, she just had to hope she wouldn't see any of the other cleaners by mistake.

Luckily Sheila spotted Teresa first, working in one of the classrooms. Sheila stood in the corridor watching her friend. Teresa had her back to the classroom door. She was bent over a waste-paper basket, emptying it. Sheila hesitated a moment, then she coughed. Teresa straightened up and turned round to see who was there.

The change in her was shocking. In place of the trim, pert, pretty, if fading, woman she'd been, Teresa looked ten years older, weary to death, and as if she hadn't washed or combed her hair for weeks. Sheila stepped forward.

'Teresa . . .'

'What do you want?'

'I have to talk to you.'

Teresa just looked at her, still hostile. Sheila couldn't bear it.

'Won't you let me explain?'

'I don't want to hear nothing you've got to say.'

Sheila felt her heart beating fast. There was a lump in her chest, she was out of breath, scared. 'I'm going to say it anyway.'

Teresa just stood, stricken. Sheila felt the lump dissolve. She was near to tears. 'I'm sorry. Honest to God I'm sorry.'

Suddenly Teresa seemed to crumble. She sat down on one of the classroom chairs. 'How has it happened, Shei?'

'I don't know.'

'How could Matty do it?'

Sheila felt helpless. 'Sometimes I think I don't know anything.' She sat down next to Teresa.

'Where have I gone wrong?' Teresa asked. 'What have I done to make him do this?'

'You've done nothing wrong. You've been a good wife.'

'I asked him, Shei. I said "Matty, is it because she's cleverer than me?"'

'It's nothing like that. Don't blame yourself. It's just something that's happened to him.'

'It's not Matty is it, doing this? Not the Matty I know.'

'People change I suppose.'

Teresa nodded. 'Matty changed when he lost his job. He just sank right down, as if the stuffing went out of him.' She managed what was almost a laugh. 'Then when he started this course he seemed to feel better. And I was glad, God help me.'

'He *was* better.' Sheila said. 'It gave him back his self-respect.'

'The course? Or her?'

'I don't know, Teresa.'

'I do. Her. He practically said as much. "She makes me feel brand-new" . . . that's what he said.'

'It wasn't your fault, see. It's happened because he was down. . . .'

Teresa started to cry. 'Don't you think I didn't know how down he was? He's felt so useless these past years. He's tried so hard to get work. You know that.'

'Yes.'

'And got knocked back. He's not a man that can be out of work. He can't stand being idle. Oh, Matty . . .' Now that Teresa's tears had started, it seemed as if they couldn't stop.

Sheila sat, holding Teresa's arm. She wasn't crying, her tears had gone. Besides, Teresa was crying enough for both of them. And she felt angry, not tearful. It wasn't right, what was happening, not right at all. She couldn't bear to see Teresa sitting there destroyed.

She couldn't help somewhere having some understanding for Matty. It must have been awful for him for the last two years. Nothing to do, nowhere to go, feeling useless. No wonder he'd been so susceptible. No wonder he'd fallen for Mo and the promise of a fresh start she offered. But it wasn't right that Teresa should suffer. Sheila put her arms round her friend. 'I have tried, you know, to make Matty see what he's done. Him and Mo. I've had it out with them.'

'Oh, Sheila. I miss him so much.' And Teresa cried again. 'I wake up in the morning and expect to find him there. I even had to go down the Social and explain ... to a kid not much older than our Stephen. My husband's left me. That's what I had to say.'

'Oh, love.'

'I think it'd be easier if he was dead. At least he wouldn't have wanted to leave me.'

Sheila walked home the long way round. She was upset and anxious, and she needed time to think. There must be something she could do to help, whatever Bobby said. And whatever names she was called. She remembered the anonymous letter she'd had ... only the one, but she wouldn't forget it. Of what it said: 'Keep out of other people's business you interfering bitch.'

Now she'd seen the state Teresa was in, this was her business.

Chapter Four

For Harry and Ralph time went slowly. Being a widower didn't suit either of them but, as Ralph said, what can't be cured must be endured, and at least they had each other. Harry wasn't quite sure how Ralph meant that but he decided not to ask.

Despite Harry's occasional grumbles they were glad enough to do their bit on Paul's crossing patrol: it gave them something to take an interest in. Then there were Harry's duties as a landlord, which he took very seriously indeed. He had decided to put the house next door up for rent when it had proved hard to sell after he and Edna had moved out of it into the bungalow, and now he enjoyed being a house owner twice over. He kept careful accounts of the rent that he collected each week from Pat or Sandra or Terry and, as far as possible, kept a keen eye on how they were treating his property.

Apart from that, Harry's major occupation was watching the doings of the other occupants of the Close, particularly the younger ones. At least Karen Grant seemed to have settled down with a steady young man, which was more than could be said for young Tracy Corkhill. There'd be plenty to keep his eye on when she got a bit older if she carried on as she'd begun.

Ralph had more to keep him occupied than Harry. He could drive the car, and he had his friendship with Madge Richmond to bring a sparkle to his eye and a spring to his step. He very much enjoyed their outings together to the seaside, or into town for a look round the shops or across the water to the Wirral to meet some of Madge's friends. Inspired by these outings, and wanting to share some of what they saw with Harry, Ralph decided to buy a camera.

As a first step, he brought home a photographic magazine, intending to look through the small ads for a second-hand bargain. Harry, seeing it on the table, picked it up suspiciously.

'What's this for?'

'I told you I was thinking of looking for a camera.'

Harry was peering at the cover picture with a mixture of fascination and disapproval.

'Look at this girl. If she had anything less on she'd be in her birthday suit.'

'It's called glamour photography.'

'Disgusting I call it.'

'That's a very respected magazine in the camera world.'

'Well I'm not having it in my house. Some of these pictures are obscene.'

'Just show me some that are obscene.'

Harry flicked over the pages, lingering over some of them. 'Look at that, you can nearly see all she's got.'

'And you're making sure you do.'

'Pan calling the kettle black.' Harry stopped, flicked back a page. 'Eh, look at this. Who does this remind you of?' Ralph looked. The girl in the bathing suit did seem vaguely familiar.

'Someone on the telly?'

'Nearer than that. Isn't it that girl who comes up here to see Terry Sullivan? Vicki something?'

'Oh, ey, Harry, you might be right.'

'I am right. So that's what they get up to. And in my house. They're only renting it you know. That makes me responsible for what happens.'

'You can't see it's your house, it's just a blank wall. Could be anywhere.'

'What about them curtains then?'

'What curtains?'

'That bedroom. Where that girl slept. Kate. Always shut, aren't they?'

'Yes, they are now you mention it.'

'This explains it, doesn't it? Who knows what's going on inside? I'm going to put a stop to this.'

'Be careful, Harry, we've got to be sure. You can get in trouble making false allegations.'

'We'll keep a lookout then. Off you go.'

'Me?'

'You're on first shift.'

'I can't just stand there.'

'Of course not. Go and offer to mow their lawn.'

'What'll you be doing?'

'Me? I'll be thinking about what to do next.'

It wasn't till the next day that their vigil was rewarded. Harry had gone into the kitchen to make a cup of tea when he spotted Vicki coming up the Close.

'Quick, give me the magazine.'

'Is it her?'

'Pound to a penny. Call her over.'

'You can't do that.'

But Harry had. 'Vicki isn't it, Vicki Cleary?'

'Hello. You're Mr . . .?'

'Cross. Terry's landlord. He's not here.'

'Maybe Pat . . .'

'He's out too. Come in our house for a cup of tea.'

'I dunno.' Ralph could read her face. What was this? Was Harry a dirty old man? Would she be safe?

Mortified, he came to Harry's rescue. 'He's quite harmless, love, really.'

'All right then.'

'As a matter of fact there's something I wanted to talk about,' said Harry when they were in the house.

'What?'

'Well . . .' Again Harry's nerve failed him, and again Ralph came to the rescue. 'I'm interested in photography, you see love.'

'Yes?' Vicki was cautious again.

'And we thought you might be able to give us some hints, knowing about it.'

'I don't know much about it.'

Harry produced the magazine. 'What's this then?'

'A magazine.'

'Page twenty-three. The glamour section.' Vicki turned the pages, looked. 'Oh. I see.'

'Is it you then?'

'Yes.'

Harry shot a triumphant glance at Ralph. 'I thought as much. It's got to stop. I'm not having these kinds of immoral goings-on in my house,' he said.

'Your house? What's that to do with it?'

'This picture. Wasn't it taken there?'

'They were done last year. Before I ever came near Brookside Close.'

'Oh.' Harry seemed almost disappointed. 'Still it's not the kind of thing a nice girl would do.'

'Look,' Vicki said. 'Why should I be ashamed of these pictures? I did them for a business contact of my brother's when they needed a model in a hurry. I needed the money.'

'They paid you then?'

'Twenty-five quid.'

Ralph was impressed. 'Not bad, eh?'

'Not good either. It took hours, and I was freezing. You can see the goose pimples.'

Harry took another look at the picture. 'That's right, you can. I bet you wouldn't like Terry to see this.'

'Are you trying to blackmail me?'

'No need for language like that.'

'You're just a dirty old man.'

The insult didn't hurt Harry. He wasn't going to be put off as easily as that. He knew how to get his revenge on Vicki, and do his public duty into the bargain. Terry Sullivan might not be quite Harry's type but he was a neighbour. It was up to Harry to let him know just what kind of a girl Vicki was.

Terry looked poker-faced when Harry showed him the photographic magazine. 'It's her, you know,' said Harry. 'She's admitted it.'

'It's her right enough.'

'I should face her with it if I was you.'

'Oh, I will.'

'You can borrow the magazine.'

'Thanks.'

Terry had the magazine behind his back when Vicki came. After she had kissed him he held it out.

'Seen this before, have you?'

Her face fell.

'He showed it you, did he?'

'You bet he did. He couldn't wait.'

'Dirty old man.'

Terry smiled. 'You're right.'

Vicki smiled too. 'You don't mind?'

'Why should I? I think you look terrific.'

'Oh Terry, that's great. He wanted to give me a fright.'

'Let's think of a way to pay him back.'

They staged their scene carefully. First they went round the house collecting every magazine they could find. Then Terry kept watch till he saw Harry in the garden. When he gave the nod to Vicki. She raised her voice deliberately.

'I'm sorry, Terry. Please forgive me.'

Terry opened the back door and pushed her through it.

'Get out, you. Get out of my house.' He appeared behind her with the pile of magazines. 'And take this lot with you. I'm not having stuff like that in my house.'

Vicki scrambled for the magazines, picked them up and put them in the bin. Then, sobbing, she went round the front. Once she was safely inside the front door she and Terry clung on to each other, stifling their giggles.

'You're sure he saw you?'

'Quite sure.'

'Just wait for the bin lid to go.'

Carefully Harry opened the bin. He took out one of the magazines and opened it quickly. Behind him, Ralph appeared with his new camera. It hadn't been out of his

52

hands ever since he'd got it: he'd been taking pictures of Harry from breakfast-time on. This one was definitely too good to miss.

'Watch the birdy, Harry,' he said.

Vicki and Terry leaned over the fence. 'So you don't read dirty books, eh?'

As Harry turned, books in hand, Ralph pressed the camera button. The shutter clicked.

'Got it,' said Ralph. 'Harry on a dirty picture.'

Damon Grant came back from his job in Torquay older, wiser and very disillusioned. After two months slaving away in a hotel kitchen for a pittance, he had been given the sack at a week's notice when a big booking had been cancelled. When he described his working conditions to Sheila, she was shocked.

'Seventy-four hours a week? In that heat? You must've been worn out.'

'I was. We all were. That's why there's accidents.' And Damon showed her the burn on his arm.

'Why did you stick it? We wouldn't have minded if you'd come home.'

'No work here is there? And I wanted to show them that people from Liverpool know how to work. You know what they call us down there, don't you?'

'What?'

'Scouse skivers.'

'That's not fair.'

'You know that, I know that, but they don't. They say there'd be work up here if people wanted it.'

'Tell Matty that.'

'So you see, I had to show them.'

'Well, you're home now.'

'And out of a job.'

Damon wasn't the only one with problems. The day he came home Sally Dinsdale appeared in Sheila's doorstep with her silent children. She was bruised and shaking.

'He's had a go at me again, Sheila. I couldn't take it any more, I've left him.' Sheila offered tea and sympathy, but this time she didn't offer a bed as she had once before. She had another idea.

'D'you remember that woman that came to talk to us about violence to women?'

'Yeah.'

'Well she was from a women's refuge. Why don't you spend the night there?'

Sally perked up. 'It'd do me for a couple of nights while I get myself sorted, wouldn't it?'

Bobby was touched by Sally's plight and offered her a lift to the refuge. But Sheila demurred. 'You can't take her, Bob.'

'Why not?'

'It's one of the rules. They won't let her in if they see a man bringing her.'

Bobby was hurt. 'I wouldn't hurt a fly, Shei, you know that. I've never raised a hand to a woman in my life.'

'I know that, but they don't. They're frightened, Bobby.' Eventually Sally went off in a taxi, intending to pretend she was going to visit an aunt. Bobby wasn't pleased.

'They're teaching you some funny ideas on that course.'

'I'm learning a bit about how the other half lives.'

'Poking your nose into other people's business . . .'

This was an old and well-worn topic. 'I suppose you mean Matty and Teresa?'

'Suppose I do?'

'Well somebody needs to, Bobby. And if you won't, I have to. If somebody doesn't intervene, they won't have a marriage left.'

'I've told you before and I'll tell you again, you're asking for trouble. If you paid more attention to your own family and less to other people, we'd all be a lot better off.'

Unknown to Bobby somebody else agreed with him. That

54

was Ken Dinsdale. Even though he treated Sally like a punchbag he missed her desperately now she wasn't there. He came to the education centre one day when the tutorial was meeting, walking into the room uninvited and un-announced.

Alun Jones spotted him first. 'Can I help you?'

Dinsdale looked round. There was no Sally, she was lying low; so he played his second card. 'Is there a Mrs Grant here?'

Sheila looked up. 'That's me.'

'Could I have word?'

'Well . . .'

'It's all right, Sheila,' Alun said, 'we've finished anyway.'

'It's very important.' Sheila had no idea who he was. Embarrassed and anxious she let him lead her into the corner of the room. He spoke softly so that none else could hear.

'I'm Ken Dinsdale.'

'Oh.' Sheila was scared. His tone was calm but the look on his face was hard.

'Where's Sally?'

'She's . . . I dunno.'

'Don't give me that.'

Sheila remembered the marks on Sally's body. Fist marks. Boot marks. And, even worse, the look on Sally's face, the look of sheer terror when she spoke of Ken. And the silent children. Indignation gave Sheila courage. 'I don't know. And if I did I wouldn't tell you.'

Dinsdale drew his fist back ever so slightly. Sheila saw his shoulder bunch under his jacket. 'Tell me or else. She's mine.'

'No, she's not. She's not your property. She's a person in her own right.'

'Don't you talk to me about Sally. It's all your fault she's left. It's you put her up to it, isn't it? Where is she?'

Luckily Alun and Matty had realized something was wrong. They came up behind Dinsdale.

'Tell him, Shei,' Matty said, edging in front of Dinsdale.
'Never.'

'It's between him and Sally isn't it?' Matty edged closer.

Dinsdale half turned to look at this unexpected ally. In that moment Alun grabbed his arms. 'Well done, Matty.'

Matty took hold of Dinsdale's shoulders. 'Walk out of here,' he said. 'And quick.'

'All right, all right. I wasn't going to hurt her.'

'You weren't going to get the chance,' said Matty.

Dinsdale was outnumbered and he knew it. He went quietly. Sheila leaned against the wall, weak with relief. Alun put an arm out to support her. 'You all right?'

'No harm done.'

'This time. Shall I run you home? You don't want to be waiting at any bus stops.'

'No,' said Sheila. Supposing Dinsdale decided to lie in wait? 'You're right. I couldn't face going home on my own. But I don't want to bother you.'

'On the contrary, it'll be a pleasure.'

Alun and Sheila got to Brookside Close just as Bobby got in from work. Alun helped Sheila out of the car and up the path. Bobby wasn't pleased to see them together. In Bobby's view Sheila had changed a lot, and not altogether for the better since she'd started on this course, and he blamed quite a lot of that on Alun Jones. He didn't mince words. 'What you doing here?'

'He gave me a lift, Bob.'

'I bet he did.'

'Mr Grant, somebody tried to beat her up.'

'Who did?'

'Sally Dinsdale's husband.'

'I'll kill him.'

'For God's sake Bobby, don't,' said Sheila.

'Where do I find him?' Bobby was already going for his coat.

'Don't do anything hasty. Talk about it first,' said Alun.

56

All Bobby's latent jealousy of Alun came to the fore. 'This is great, isn't it? Some egg-head telling me what's best for me own wife.'

'Don't you start,' said Sheila, angry and upset. 'You call me "Me own wife", you threaten violence . . . You're as bad as Ken Dinsdale.'

Bobby was hurt. 'How can you say that?'

'I didn't mean it. Not like that. Only . . . I don't want any more trouble.'

'She'd get a lot more out of a cup of tea and some caring words than all this shouting,' Alun said.

It was like a red rag to a bull to Bobby. 'Don't tell me what to do for my Sheila,' he said.

Sheila looked at Alun. 'I'll be all right on my own.'

'You sure?'

'It's best.'

When he'd gone, Bobby and Sheila looked at each other, both of them upset by the angry words. 'Oh Bob . . .'

Bobby was bewildered and distressed. 'I only want what's best,' he said.

'I know you do.'

'But you're different. You're never in, not since you started this course.'

'I am in. Just not all the time like I used to be.'

'And you meet all these new people . . .'

Sheila went to him. 'They're not important, you are.'

Bobby held out his arms. 'Come here, girl.'

'Oh, Bobby, it was awful. I was really frightened.'

'Just keep out of it, queen. If you don't, where's it going to end?'

Heather's wedding preparations were getting on well except for one thing. It was the height of the season at the hotel and her mother couldn't get away. If Heather had any fears that it might also indicate that her mother wasn't altogether pleased at a wedding only months after the end of the relationship with Tom, she kept them to herself.

Nick's children reacted to the prospect of their father having a new wife in different ways. Adam was absolutely delighted and didn't attempt to conceal the fact. As far as Heather could tell, Scott seemed to accept whatever happened. In any case he kept his thoughts to himself. Ruth was the difficult one. Heather made a special effort to be nice to her and seemed to be having some success, though it was hard to be certain, as Ruth's mood could change from one day to the next.

One day she arrived on Heather's doorstep in what was definitely a bad mood. 'Is dad in?' she asked.

Nick appeared behind Heather. 'Ruth! This is a surprise.'

'It shouldn't be,' said Ruth.

'Oh my goodness . . .' Nick shook his head in exasperation with himself. 'I'm sorry, I said I'd pick you up at my flat, didn't I? I didn't go there, I came straight here from work.'

'Half an hour I stood there. It's typical.'

'Memory's not his strong point, is it?' said Heather. 'I only hope he remembers to turn up for the wedding.'

'Oh, he will,' said Ruth. 'It's not you that's the problem.'

'What is?'

'How should I know?'

Heather had learned the hard way not to tangle with Ruth when she was in one of her awkward moods. 'I'll put the kettle on,' she said.

'It wasn't just me,' Ruth said to Nick. 'Charlie was waiting. He said you'd promised.'

'Where is he now?'

'It's all right,' said Ruth. 'I sorted him out.'

'I've still not met Charlie, remember?' said Heather, coming back in. 'Why didn't you bring him round here with you?'

Ruth glanced at Nick. 'I'm not sure dad would have liked it.'

'Don't cause trouble, Ruth,' said Nick.

'When am I going to meet him then?' Heather asked.

'I've said. At the wedding.'

Annabelle, perhaps giving up hope of ever being the mother of the bride in her own right, was delighted to do everything she could to help with Heather's preparations. One day Heather took time off work and she and Annabelle went shopping together.

Heather was determined to have nothing but the best. In the euphoria of her new promotion and the joy of the relationship with Nick, she didn't care how much money she spent. Annabelle and she shopped all morning and then had lunch in the most expensive restaurant in town, before starting on more shopping. Heather bought underwear, nightwear, new bed linen and, most important of all, her dress. She went in six shops and tried on about twenty dresses before she found the one she wanted. It was soft and creamy and fitted like a glove. Annabelle was entranced. 'You look marvellous, Heather. You'll be the perfect bride.'

'You don't think it's too much? For second time round?'

'It's perfect. Just perfect. You'll look lovely.'

'Don't tell anyone what it's like then. Especially not Nick. I want to surprise him.'

The only dark moment of the day was caused by Harry Cross. He came across to Heather's with a wedding present: the same set of glasses he'd given when he thought she was going to marry Tom.

'These seem familiar.'

'Always come in handy.'

'Thank you, Harry.'

'I expect you were going to call over.'

Heather knew what he wanted: an invitation. 'Not exactly. Er . . . we're not inviting many people. Just family mainly.'

'Isn't Annabelle Collins going?'

'Yes, but . . .'

'But I'm not good enough.'

'I'm sorry. But we had to draw the line somewhere. With having the reception at home.'

It took a minute or two to sink in. Then Harry was furious.

'I don't expect it'll last long anyway. With you both divorced. Him with children too.'

'I don't see what that's got to do with it.'

'You're marrying him on the rebound anyway.'

'I'm not. Oh . . . you couldn't begin to understand.' Heather handed the glasses back. 'Here you are. I don't want them.'

'Come in handy again then, won't they? I give it six months. At the outside. Six months, that's all.'

Things between Pat and Sandra were no better. Pat was desperate for a reconciliation and Sandra's birthday seemed as good a time as any other. He consulted Terry about a suitable gift.

'What d'you think about a roof rack? Not much room in that car.'

Terry was sarcastic. 'It's dead romantic, that. I can just hear her saying, "Oh what a lovely roof rack."'

'How about a fancy nightie then?'

'Not exactly subtle is it?'

'What, then?'

'Scent.'

'It's not original, is it?'

'No. But it's safe.'

Pat went to town determined to find something more exciting than scent. He came back with some highly expensive perfume. And some very glossy wrapping paper.

Sandra was working the day of her birthday, so Pat got his present in first. She was delighted. 'Och, Pat, that's lovely.'

'Aren't you going to put it on.'

'Not to go to work.'

60

'What's wrong with smelling nice at work?'

'Not quite the thing, is it? Don't want to overpower the patients.'

'Are you sure you like it?'

'Oh, Pat, don't pester.'

Pat's spirits didn't improve when Terry came downstairs with his present. 'Here you are: Happy Birthday.' Sandra unwrapped her parcel. 'It's only scent I know,' said Terry. 'But it always comes in useful.'

Sandra was amused. 'I suppose you racked your brains for ages, did you?'

Terry was honest. 'It was all I could think of. The old stand-by, isn't it?' Pat could have killed him.

He spent a miserable day until Sandra came back home that afternoon. She brought with her another present: some black leather flat shoes. 'Look what Tony bought me.'

'He's meant to be a colleague, for goodness sake.'

'So?'

'So what's he buying you shoes for?'

'I'm a nurse. Feet are important.'

'They're not exactly sexy are they?' said Terry, trying to help.

'But useful,' said Sandra. 'Very appropriate for a nurse.' Sometimes Pat thought he couldn't win.

He certainly didn't think he could win over the business of the campaign against Mr Cribbs-Baker. Sandra seemed determined to go ahead with it no matter what. She and Tony had finally finished looking through the case histories. They'd compiled a dossier of what they thought to be questionable cases and Tony was going to present it to the general manager. He telephoned Sandra at home with the result of the meeting. Pat was there, pretending not to listen.

'That was Tony,' Sandra said when she put the phone down.

'You don't say,' said Pat sarcastically.

For once Sandra didn't rise to the bait. 'He's just been in to see the general manager.'

'You said he was going to.'

'Yes. Well, he's been knocked back.'

Her evident disappointment made Pat gentle. 'How?'

'The manager reckons that if we've got a case at all it's about Cribbs-Baker's ethics, not his competence.'

Pat stifled an impulse to say, 'I told you so,' and tried instead: 'What does that mean?'

'It means that if we still want to do anything about it, we've got to take it to the General Medical Council in London. It'll take ages. And cause a big stink.'

'Doesn't look too hopeful, then?'

'Not hopeful at all. They look after their own, that lot.'

'Not worth it, then?'

'It looks like this might be the end of the road.'

Pat's hopes rose. If Sandra gave up the campaign that would mean the end of the relationship with Hurrell. He'd be in with a chance again. Perhaps things between him and Sandra could get back to where they were before this business started.

But his hopes were short-lived. By the time Tony Hurrell came round to discuss the situation Sandra's spirits had rallied. She had enough determination for both of them.

'No good going further,' Tony said.

'We've got to go further. We can't stop now.'

Tony was getting cold feet. 'What difference will it make? I mean, what's he done? Performed a few operations that may not have been necessary. How're we going to prove it?'

'These aren't just operations. These are women having their wombs removed. You can't even begin to understand what that means.'

'If we take this to the General Council it'll become a completely different ballgame, right? It could cost us both our careers, you know that don't you?'

'I don't believe this,' said Sandra. 'This man is cutting up women's bodies and you want to forget about it. We can't give up now.'

62

'When you put it like that . . .'

'Are you with me?'

'I suppose so.'

When Pat found that Sandra was still determined to go ahead with the campaign, he couldn't believe his ears.

'I thought you'd given up on it.'

'They've not beaten us yet.'

'You'll be wasting your time. It's only a difference of opinion on how to operate.'

'It's a risk we have to take.' All Pat's jealousy surfaced again. ' "We." That's it, isn't it? That's what it's all about. You wouldn't be so keen if you didn't fancy him.'

'Don't be so childish.'

'You might be fooling yourself, Sand, but you can't fool me. I've got eyes in my head. I know what's going on.'

'You disgust me, you and your suspicions. What I'm doing is right. You should be supporting it, not knocking it. What sort of a friend d'you call yourself?'

It was another sleepless night for Pat.

Chapter Five

Heather woke early on the morning of her wedding day. She sat up, savouring the day ahead. This was the last time she'd have this room to herself: tomorrow Nick would be here. And every morning after that. Someone to bring her a cup of tea, someone to talk to, someone to lean on. She couldn't wait.

Joyce came over early to help her get ready. She cooed over Heather's dress as Heather arranged a bowl of flowers on the bedside table. 'You'll look gorgeous.'

'You don't look so bad yourself. I bet that cost a bit.'

'What if it did? I know a special occasion when I see one.'

The Collins were up early too, looking after their guest. They'd offered a bed to Teddy, Heather's cousin, over from Ireland for the occasion. Annabelle couldn't believe how much breakfast he could eat. She'd run out of bread and bacon, Paul would have to make do with cereal. She hoped the caterers Heather was using had provided adequately. Some of them had a tendency to cut down so as to increase profits. Guest or no guest she would gladly have done the catering and was still a bit disappointed that she hadn't been asked.

Paul wasn't thinking about whether there'd be enough food, it was the drink he had doubts about if Teddy went on as he'd begun. Paul surveyed his whisky decanter ruefully. Teddy certainly could get through the whisky. It was a good job he was only staying for two nights.

Over at Nick's flat the children were helping their father to get ready for his big day. Adam was by a long way the most excited. He'd taken to Heather from the moment he'd first met her and was delighted that she was finally going to be his step-mother. He polished his shoes till he nearly wore a hole in them and combed his hair twenty times in an attempt to get the fringe to lie flat. He checked his appearance anxiously with Ruth. 'Do I look all right?'

'Fine.' The six years' difference in age and the rather lackadaisical ways of their mother made Ruth feel maternal towards Adam. These days she was at odds with most of the world most of the time, but not with Adam. 'You look great.'

Ruth herself hadn't gone to anything like as much trouble with her appearance. She had very mixed feelings about this whole event. Nevertheless she agreed to wear a flower on her blouse to please her father. Ruth would do a lot to please her father. Scott, as ever, did what was easiest. If his dad wanted him to wear a sports jacket he'd wear one. Scott didn't much mind what he did so long as people left him alone. . . .

Joyce helped Heather fix a flower on the front of her dress. 'You look great.'

'Thanks.'

'All the time I've known you I've waited for you to be happy. It's lovely to see it.'

'It's lovely to *be* it.' And, feeling it, Heather felt the tears rise in her eyes. Gently Joyce passed her a paper tissue. 'Hey, you'll make your mascara run. You're supposed to be happy, remember.'

'I am.'

'Sure?'

'Quite sure.'

There was quite a reception committee waiting when Heather stepped into the Close. Sheila carried Claire out to wave to the bride. Damon got out of bed specially to see what was going on. Paul and Annabelle, already dressed in their best for the reception, came to their front

65

door. Inside the bungalow Harry, who'd been keeping a lookout since morning, called to Ralph to join him.

'They're going.'

'She looks very nice,' said Ralph.

'Hmmmm,' was all Harry would say.

Nick and the children were waiting at the register office with Heather's father and Charlie, Nick's witness. Adam was well prepared with a bag of rice. He was the one who spotted Heather's approaching car. 'Dad, she's here. Get inside quick or you'll see her.'

The ceremony was short and sweet. Ten minutes later, it was done. Heather was Nick's wife. There were kisses and congratulations all round, and Adam, against the rules, threw a tiny bit of his rice. Some of it stuck in Heather's hair and Nick, picking it out, took the opportunity to kiss her again.

'Welcome to married life,' he said.

Heather's father shook Nick's hand. 'Welcome to the family.'

Joyce kissed them both. 'Congratulations. I hope you'll be very happy.'

And if Ruth held back nobody noticed.

Back at Brookside Close the wedding party was joined by the Collins and the Grants. Annabelle inspected the lunch and found it wanting. 'I'd be careful of the chicken legs,' she said to Paul. 'They don't look properly cooked to me.' Paul tried one later and thought it was delicious but he didn't tell Annabelle that.

Sheila introduced Claire to Heather's father, who wondered if he might hope for a granddaughter one of these days. Paul talked cricket with Adam, and Damon and Teddy became instant friends and self-appointed wine waiters. As the day wore on, toasts were drunk. First, of course, to the bride and groom, then to Joyce and Charlie, then to the children. After that it was open season and everybody drank toasts to everybody else.

And again, if Ruth held back it wasn't noticed.

The only disappointment for Heather was Charlie. She'd heard about him from Nick and from Ruth: he was Nick's best friend from years back and she'd been very much looking forward to meeting him. But he was rather distant and difficult to get to know, as if he lived in a world of his own. The only person he really talked to was Joyce.

'How long d'you and Nick know each other?' she asked.

'Since university. Nineteen sixty-four.'

'Are you in the architects' department too, like Nick?'

Charlie let out a brief laugh. 'No. That's not my thing at all.'

'What do you do?'

'Lecturer.'

'What subject?'

'I just fill in at the poly sometimes.'

'Oh.' Frankly Joyce couldn't see what Nick saw in Charlie. She said as much to Heather. 'If you have any idea for cosy dinner parties don't ring me.'

'I doubt it'll arise,' said Heather. 'From what I know he's not exactly the socializing type.'

The party began to break up and Heather went in search of Nick. 'He's in the garden talking to Ruth,' said Adam. 'They're always having little talks.'

'Perhaps you and me'll have little talks now,' said Heather. 'In a way I'm going to be your mother.'

'All right,' said Adam.

Nick was standing at the end of the garden, deep in talk with Ruth. He turned at Heather's call. 'People are going.' He gave Ruth's shoulder a squeeze and came in to say goodbye to his guests.

At last everyone went and the caterers had cleared up. Nicholas and Heather were left alone together. But Teddy hadn't finished with them yet.

They'd had a tiring day and they definitely wanted an early night. Heather used her most expensive bubble bath and put on her special nightie. Nick was turning down the new sheets on the bed when she went into the bedroom.

'Well Mrs Black . . . How does it feel to be Mrs Black?'

'It feels . . . wonderful.'

'And it's going to get better.'

They got into bed. 'What the . . .' Nick drew his feet up sharply and then scrabbled under the sheets. He came up with a handful of grains of rice.

'It's Adam. Just wait till I get him.'

Heather was laughing. 'I'd put money on it being Teddy.'

It didn't spoil anything.

The only people who didn't enjoy the day were Pat and Sandra. They were invited to the wedding but they didn't make it. The trouble began over Pat's ill-fated birthday present. He sniffed Sandra's neck as they were about to leave for Heather's.

'Why aren't you wearing that perfume I bought you?'

'I forgot.'

'Great. I get you the best stuff I can find and you forget to put it on.'

'Leave me alone for goodness sake!'

Pat's fears came back in a rush. 'It'd be different, wouldn't it, if Tony Hurrell'd bought it for you? You'd never stop wearing it then, would you? Like those shoes. It's a wonder you're not wearing them now.'

'Are you going to leave me alone?'

'I only want you to wear my present.'

'We're only living together. You don't own me.'

'I don't want to own you. I just want us to be a couple. I wish this was our wedding.'

'No chance.'

'Sandra.'

'Not now. Or ever.'

Pat reached out for her. 'Don't say that.'

'Get off me.' Sandra pushed him away. Pat raised his hand, then, angry though he was, stopped at the sight of Sandra's face.

'I'm sorry.'

'Too late to be sorry isn't it? I've been here before you
68

know, with a man that used his fists. I'll not make that mistake again.'

Paul's enthusiasm for the crossing patrol had been rather dampened by his encounter with PC Moonan. Obviously different tactics were necessary. He tried to contact Kathleen Monaghan again, but that was easier said than done. All he could discover was that she was 'out' and messages asking her to ring him were to no avail. Then she rang up and arranged to come round. Paul put a tie on for the occasion and Annabelle brewed some real coffee. She'd show Mrs Monaghan that she knew how things should be done.

Paul greeted Kathleen warmly. 'Nice to see you.'

'Nice to be here. Looked as if I wouldn't make it last week.'

'Why not?'

'I was up in court, that's why. I thought they were going to send me down.'

'Down?' Paul hoped he'd misunderstood. He carefully avoided looking at Annabelle's face.

'To prison. For obstructing the highway.' Now Paul didn't need to look at Annabelle's face. He could tell how she felt from the way she suddenly froze, holding the coffee pot in mid-air. Kathleen, however, seemed imperturbable. 'Still I got away with it this time. They only fined me thirty quid.'

Paul tried to change the subject. 'I was wondering if we could get together to organize some crossing patrols in other areas. Mobilize some people.'

'Patrols do no good, we've got to block the roads. Sitting on our bums if need be.'

Paul's enthusiasm was distinctly on the wane. 'But it's against the law, Mrs Monaghan. You've just been fined.'

Annabelle could keep quiet no longer. 'And presumably if you keep it up you'll end up in prison.'

Kathleen could hardly keep the scorn out of her voice. 'No presume about it, I would. We all would.'

'But my husband's already had one warning. He can't take any risks.'

Kathleen was impatient. 'You get nowhere if you don't take risks. Mr Collins, are you serious about helping these children?'

'I am.'

'Then you'll have to break the law for it. Whatever happens.'

Annabelle went into the attack as soon as Kathleen had left. 'You can't get involved in breaking the law, Paul.'

'I don't intend to.'

'But if you do what she's suggesting you will.'

'I'll think of something else. Some other tactics.'

'If she'll listen. She's got the bit between her teeth.'

Paul agreed but didn't want to admit it. 'Annabelle, I can't just drop this campaign because the going might get rough. I feel very strongly about it.'

'I know you do. But it's rather an awkward time, isn't it? They'll be keeping an eye on us you know, to see if I'm suitable to be a magistrate.'

'I'll be careful, Anna.'

'I hope you will. Because if you don't you could wreck my chances, couldn't you?'

Sally Dinsdale didn't dare go to the Return to Learn group after she heard what had happened to Sheila. She wouldn't venture out of the hostel. Conditions there might be cramped, but at least she was safe. The next week Matty didn't go either. That left only Sheila, Alun and Mo. It wasn't a comfortable atmosphere. Alun suggested cancelling the class.

'You can choose, but I don't really see much point.'

Mo didn't want to be left with Sheila. 'I think I'll just go home.'

The memory of Teresa's tearful face gave Sheila courage. 'Mo, I'd like a word with you.'

Alun had a good idea of what was going to happen. He made himself scarce. 'I'll be in my office if you need me.'

There was a silence when he'd gone. Sheila and Mo looked at each other. Mo spoke first.

'I don't want a fight. I know what you're going to say, but you're wasting your time.'

'I think you should at least listen.'

'Why? There's nothing you can say can alter anything.'

'I've got to try and get through to you.'

'I'm sick of you and your morality. It's between Matty and me. We'll sort ourselves out.'

'There's more than you involved. What about Matty's kids?'

'That's up to him, isn't it?'

Sheila sighed. There seemed no way of getting through. She rubbed her head wearily. 'I don't know how to explain.'

'Why should I listen? You just hate me.'

'No I don't. I just don't understand you.'

'I love Matty. That's all there is to understand.'

'What about Teresa? I've been to see her . . . it'd make your heart bleed.' Mo was silent now, listening. 'She's stood by him all this time, the years out of work. Now she's destroyed. She doesn't deserve any of this.' Mo's head was down so Sheila couldn't see her face but she sensed she was getting through. Sheila began to soften. Now that Mo had stopped defending herself she seemed pathetic rather than wicked. Sheila even began to feel sorry for her.

Then she remembered the last sight of Teresa standing in the classroom doorway, mop in one hand, rubbing her eyes with the other. She'd looked so sad, so down, so despairing. Sheila had to do something to help, she owed her. What could she say that would convince Mo?

'Think about Teresa. Not "Matty's wife" . . . Teresa. I know you've only seen her the once and that was when she was angry, but she was only like that because she's frightened. The real Teresa, the one I know, isn't like that. The Teresa I know is an ordinary woman, just like you and me. Can you do this to her?'

Mo was silent, thinking. Then she spoke, sadly, and Sheila knew she'd won.

'You know where Matty is today?'

'No?'

'Down south. To look for work. And somewhere for us to live. We were going to have a fresh start, see.'

Sheila said nothing. Mo managed a twist of the lips that was meant to pass for a smile. 'He thinks he's going to find a country cottage. With roses round the door.'

'I'm sorry.' Sheila turned to go. Mo stopped her. 'There's just one thing . . .'

'Yes?'

'Did you get a letter? Anonymous?'

'Telling me to keep out? It was you?'

Mo nodded. 'Yes. I'm sorry.'

'That's . . . all right.'

Sheila couldn't face going home straight away. She walked shakily along the corridor to Alun's office. He could see at once that something was wrong. 'Coffee?' he said.

'I could do with a sit-down.'

'You take on too much,' he said. 'You can't be responsible for all the world.'

'Not all the world, no. But some things.'

'Sheila, you need protecting from yourself.'

'I'm all right. Just a bit tired.'

'You need more support at home. More understanding.' Sheila felt uncomfortable. She knew very well what Alun was getting at. Alun had already made it plain that he didn't like Bobby any more than Bobby liked him. Sometimes it felt as if they were fighting over her, with Bobby wanting to keep her home, just a wife and mother, same as she'd always been, and Alun encouraging her to carry on with her education and begin to live for herself. He was at it again now.

'You could go far, Sheila, if only you'd believe in yourself. You've got brains. You really should try for O levels next year.'

Sheila resisted the impulse to say that Bobby wouldn't like it. That would just be giving Alun another chance to go on about Bobby. It didn't help that there was some truth in what he said. Bobby had encouraged Karen to pass her exams and go to university but he didn't want it for his wife. Not if it affected his home comforts.

Sheila felt disloyal even to be thinking such things. She loved Bobby and he loved her. They'd got a good marriage and four good kids. Why couldn't she be satisfied with that?

Alun was still trying to persuade her. 'You need a break. Something to take your mind off things. Remember that weekend course I told you about?'

'Yes.'

'There are still some places left. Why don't you come?'

Sheila was very tempted. But then she remembered the snag. This wasn't a course for the whole class: she'd be on her own with Alun. She was sure Bobby was wrong about Alun fancying her, but still, better safe than sorry. 'No thanks,' she said firmly.

She wondered whether to tell Bobby that she'd spoken to Mo but she didn't get a chance. Bobby had plenty of other things to worry about.

A letter had come, summoning him to London to appear before the National Executive Committee of the union. They had refused to support him in making the strike at Bragg's Engineering official and now they wanted an explanation of why he had done so without their authority. He was well aware that if he didn't make a good showing it could cost him his job.

Sheila took his suit to the cleaners, ironed his shirt and bought him a new tie. Beyond that there wasn't much she could do except keep her fingers crossed.

Bobby arrived at the ETWU Head Office in good time. He sat outside the meeting room and watched the regional representatives go in. Tom Coates, the man from Merseyside, had known Bobby for years but he hardly managed a nod as he swept by. It was clear whose side he was on. Things weren't going to be easy for Bobby.

When he was called Bobby took his seat at the end of the table as the charge was read.

'. . . You went ahead and sanctioned this strike at Bragg's Engineering while failing to hold a ballot under the '84 Act.' That might be true but it wasn't fair.

'Maybe there was no ballot, but I had support on the district committee,' Bobby said.

'What d'you mean, maybe?' said Coates. 'There wasn't a ballot when the rules say there should've been. You had no right to make that strike official.'

After that, things went from bad to worse. Without Coates on his side Bobby didn't have a chance. After half an hour he was sent out to wait whilst the committee considered the matter.

It was one of the worst half hours of Bobby's life. What could he say to Sheila if he lost his job? Claire was only a baby still, he had her to think of. It would break Sheila's heart if she had to leave Brookside Close. Bobby reminded himself there were a lot of people much worse off, but that didn't help. He'd been a fool.

He went back into the meeting resolved to play safe. But what the president said really got up his nose. 'We want you to give us an undertaking today that we are not going to have any recurrence of this kind of action . . .'

Bobby was on his feet at once. 'All I've done is what I was elected to do . . . look after fellows in my union . . . our union. Am I supposed to rat on them because you want to fix up a national deal that'll give more power to the union?'

The president was angry now. 'See sense can't you, Bobby? If we can get a national agreement we'll get better pay and conditions for all our members. Is it worth risking that for a load of militants?'

'That's it, isn't it? That's what you really think. The lads at Bragg's are up there in Liverpool, out of sight. So

74

you just give them a label and get on lining your own pockets.'

Coates' fist on the table silenced even Bobby. 'You've gone too far . . .' He appealed to the president. 'I think we should teach him a lesson.'

The president was more conciliatory. 'I think you're saying things you'll regret, Bobby. You've had your say, blown off steam . . . let's say no more about it.'

'I've done exactly what I was elected for. Bragg's lads asked me for help and I answered them.'

'The strike's got no hope. And it's costing the union strike pay it can ill afford for a dispute that can't be won.'

Bobby was disgusted. 'I think you lot are more interested in buying carpets for this place than anything else.'

The president was firm. 'Mr Grant, do you accept to give the undertaking we requested and receive an admonishment?'

'No.'

After another awful half hour on the hard chair in the hall Bobby was summoned in for the verdict. It was a suspended sentence: decision postponed for a week; time to think.

Ken Dinsdale hadn't finished with Sheila. He was still missing Sally like hell. He was lonely, there was nobody to wash his clothes and cook his meals, nobody to comfort him in bed. And nobody to take his temper out on.

He was determined to get her back, and he had a pretty good idea that Sheila knew where she was. And if she didn't, Sally knew where Sheila was and might come and see her. He took up watch at the end of the Close.

Sheila had noticed his car a couple of times before she recognized who it was sitting in it. As soon as she realized, she shot back into the house, heart thumping, and closed the door firmly. This would happen when Bobby was away facing the Executive Committee. Sheila had enough to worry about wondering if he'd come back without his job. She could do without Ken Dinsdale.

For two days she watched Ken watching her. Then she'd had enough. Sheila was enough of a judge of people to know that bullies are often cowards. She checked that there were people around in the Close for her to feel safe. It was all right: Paul was doing his garden, Billy Corkhill painting his new garage. Taking a deep breath Sheila walked across to Dinsdale's car.

Nervously he stubbed out his cigarette as Sheila approached. She didn't give him a chance to say anything.

'It's no good hanging around. Sally won't come. She knows you're here.'

'Where is she?'

'There's no need for you to know that.'

'She's my wife.'

'Pity you didn't think about that when you were blacking her eyes. And hitting the kids.'

Dinsdale tried bullying. 'Tell me where she is or I'll black your eyes.'

'Don't you try.' Sheila sounded braver than she felt. She wasn't sorry to see Damon walking across the Close to see what was going on.

'I need her.'

'Should have thought of that before, shouldn't you?' Damon was nearer now. Dinsdale switched his car engine on. 'All right, I'm going now. But not for long. I haven't finished with you yet, Sheila Grant. Wait and see.'

Chapter Six

Having no job was getting Billy Corkhill down. He'd tried all ways to get work, writing letters, phoning, going in person. But every time the reply was the same. 'Sorry mate, nothing doing.' That is, if he got any reply at all.

Sometimes he was asked what had happened to his last job. He was a bit nervous of explaining but when he did people were usually sympathetic. 'I hit this teacher, see. He was carrying on with my daughter. She was only fifteen.'

'I don't blame you, mate. I'd have done the same. Worse. I'd've killed the bastard.' But still nobody offered him any work.

Billy did his best to keep busy. He'd done all the jobs he could think of around the house, even Doreen couldn't think of anything else she wanted doing. He'd finished off building the garage with Jimmy's bricks. He'd even dug the garden. He'd never bothered with the garden when they'd been living with his mother and didn't think he'd take to one, but in fact it was a godsend. Anything to keep him out from under Doreen's feet.

He'd given up even thinking about how they were doing for money, he left all that to Doreen. Since she'd had a credit card she hadn't asked him for much. She was doing extra hours as a receptionist for Mr Howman, the dentist for whom she worked, and she told Billy she was managing so he let her get on with it.

One day Billy came in from one of the fruitless job searches to a bit of good news. It didn't look good news at first, just another letter which he expected would be one of the usual rejections. But when he read it his hopes began to rise. 'See here, Doe. Have a read of this.'

The letter was from somebody called Julian Tyler. 'Look, there's his name printed on the notepaper, looks like he owns the firm. Industrial Maintenance it's called.'

Doe was excited but sceptical. 'Why should he write to you?'

'It says why here. "I admire your brave defence of your daughter's honour. It speaks well for your character. If you will telephone I may have an offer to discuss." He must've seen my name in the paper. Or somebody's been talking.'

Doreen practically dragged him across the room to the telephone. 'Go on then.' She held his hand whilst he dialled. He got through to the switchboard and asked for Mr Tyler. 'Must be a big firm if they've got a switchboard,' whispered Doe. 'Tell them William Corkhill.'

Mr Tyler was delighted to hear from Billy, and keen to meet him. He arranged to call round that evening on his way home from work.

As soon as Billy put the phone down Doreen went into action with the hoover and the spray polish. She thrust a duster at Billy.

'Come on, we've got to get this place straight.'

'No need for that,' said Billy. 'He's not come to see if we've done the dusting.'

'How d'you know?' said Doreen. 'That's probably why he wants to come round . . . see if you come from a decent home.'

Billy caught her anxiety. 'What d'you think he'll ask? What shall I ask him?'

'Just put a clean shirt on. And have a shave. Then you'll be all right.'

Mr Tyler appeared promptly at six o'clock as he had promised. Doreen made a mental note to point out to Billy that time-keeping would be important if he got a job with him. Mr Tyler began by offering his sympathy over what had happened to Tracy. 'Terrible thing for a young girl to be taken advantage of like that. She'll probably bear the scars for the rest of her life.'

Doreen caught Billy's eye and then looked away. It hadn't really been like that at all. Although Tracy had been only fifteen when her affair with Peter Montague had come to light it was pretty clear that she'd been as keen on him as he was on her. Still, if Mr Tyler wanted to think that Tracy had been an innocent victim let him think it. Doreen certainly wasn't going to put him right. Not if he was in a position to offer Billy a job.

It turned out that Mr Tyler did indeed own Industrial Maintenance, and that he had firm views on how it should be run.

'I've no time for unions or any of that rubbish. I only employ people I've chosen. They're answerable only to me.'

'That'll suit William,' said Doreen. 'Only last Christmas he walked through a picket line to install machinery for his firm.'

'And fine thanks I got,' said Billy. 'The sack.'

'It was a great wrong,' said Mr Tyler. 'But I've come to put it right. I've come to offer you a job. How does maintenance supervisor sound?'

Billy could hardly contain his delight. Doe didn't try to. After they'd expressed their thanks, Mr Tyler explained what was involved.

'We hire out plant and machinery all over the north-west. There's a team of five maintenance men to cover the region. I want someone who can organize them and be on hand in case we have an emergency somewhere.'

'What kind of an emergency?'

'Supposing a piece of equipment breaks down in, say, Preston, and nobody could go. You'll be the extra one. You'd get a company car, of course. With the use for your own private journeys.' This was getting better and better as far as Doreen was concerned. It'd be like having two cars. Billy was more down to earth. 'So I might be called out any time like?'

'Yes. I hope you don't go out much at night?' Doreen wasn't sure what this was about but she was determined to give Billy a good character. 'Not much chance, not with two kids. He just goes for a pint with his brother sometimes. They're a close family.'

'Have to go easy on the pints,' said Tyler. 'Lose your licence and you're no good to me.'

'No chance of that,' said Billy.

'Still, everybody needs to get out. I'll fix you up with a pager . . . one of those bleepers like doctors have . . . so we can keep in touch.'

Doreen laughed. 'I'll be able to keep track of where he is.'

'I'm sure you don't need to, Mrs Corkhill.'

'Not really. He's a lovely husband.'

'And a fine father.'

When he'd gone, Doreen and Billy danced round the room for joy.

'Two hundred and fifty, plus ovvies,' said Billy. 'And a car.'

'And a bleeper. Better keep our Rod away from that.'

'It seems too good to be true.'

'Everything's turned out all right. I told you it would. Oh, Billy, I can't believe it.'

'You will when we get the car.'

Harry had decided it was about time he learnt to drive. The car was his, there was no reason why he shouldn't get the benefit. He'd bought it on the understanding that Ralph would be the chauffeur and they'd go about together. That had worked out fine until Madge Richmond had come along but it wasn't working out any more. These days Ralph and Madge and the car were always off somewhere, leaving Harry stuck at home on his own.

He thought of the ideal way to get a lesson and to get a bit of female company. He'd ask Madge to teach him. She could hardly refuse after all the jaunts in the car she'd had and all the cups of tea she'd drunk in his house. And Ralph'd have a taste of his own medicine. He'd find out what it was like to be stuck at home on his own.

80

Harry cleaned the car himself. He wanted it to look its best when he was behind the wheel. He was just giving it a final polish when Ralph came to the door of the bungalow with a smile on his face.

'Bad news, Harry.'

'What?'

'That was Madge on the phone. She's got a cold. She's not coming.'

Harry would have kicked the blasted car if he hadn't been afraid of doing himself an injury. 'What am I going to do now?'

'Have to give it a miss won't you?'

'I'll do no such thing. Seeing as it's your girlfriend that's let me down, you'll have to take me instead.'

'No chance.'

'In that case . . .' And Harry got into the driver's seat.

Ralph's smile faded fast. 'I'm not coming.'

Harry started the engine. 'I'll have to go on my own then.'

Ralph was getting anxious. 'Don't be daft, Harry, it's against the law. You'll be banned.'

'How can I be banned if I've not got a licence?' asked Harry. He put the car into gear. It lurched forward in a kangaroo hop and stalled only an inch from the Collins' car. Ralph ran forward. 'Are you mad? Look what you nearly did.'

Harry was breathing fast. 'Give over. I was in full control.'

Damon Grant, walking up the Close, had seen what had happened. 'Practising stunt driving are we?'

Harry snorted. 'Everyone thinks he's a funny man around here.'

'Well I don't,' said Ralph. 'I just want a peaceful life, but I can't have one 'cause of this lunatic.'

Damon put on one of his innocent smiles. 'Are lunatics allowed to drive?'

'This one isn't, but he's trying,' said Ralph.

Harry was definitely not amused. 'Well if you won't

81

take me,' he said, 'what choice have I got?' And he started the engine again. Ralph was cornered. 'Wait a minute, Harry. Let's discuss it, shall we?'

'There's nothing to discuss.'

'Look, if I go with you it's only for a bit, right?'

'Right.'

Sitting in the front seat whilst Harry drove wasn't a happy experience for Ralph. More than once he thought his last hour had come. But he didn't utter a word until they drew up again in the Close. Knowing Harry's habit of waving his hands about on an argument he hadn't wanted to take the risk. But once the car was safely stationary he let Harry have it.

'D'you know what thirty miles an hour speed limit's for? It's to stop you going over thirty. It doesn't mean you must stick at thirty no matter what.'

'I didn't.'

'You did. Even roundabouts. You took everything all at thirty.'

'I was following the fellow in front.'

'He was trying to get away from you, Harry.'

After that it was back to basics. Ralph sat Harry down in the bungalow lounge with three plastic cups at his feet, labelled A, B and C. 'See them, Harry. Accelerator, Brake and Clutch. Got it?'

'I'm not stupid.'

Ralph sighed. He couldn't afford to offend Harry too much, not when it came to the car. He wouldn't put it past Harry to stop him and Madge having the use of it if he didn't get his own way. 'Let's try starting, eh, Harry. Look in the mirror.'

'What for?'

'To see what's coming up behind.'

'In here?'

'On the road.'

'I'll never learn here. I need the real thing. Let's go out.'

But Ralph had learned his lesson. 'Never again. I won't be able to sleep as it is. I'll have nightmares . . . you in a lorry on the motorway.'

Harry didn't see the joke. 'Is all this because I went at thirty miles an hour?'

'You could say that.'

Matty came back from his trip south really made up with himself. He couldn't wait to tell Mo all about it. She met him off the coach and they walked towards Abercrombie Square. It had become one of their favourite haunts.

'It's a different world down there,' he told her. 'In the country but only half an hour from London. And there's work. Just think, if we go I could do the "Access" course in Hertford *and* get a job.'

'They say the price of houses down there is terrible.'

'Not all of them. There's this cottage in the country we could have. I haven't actually seen it but I can imagine it. Our very own country cottage.'

Matty was too full of himself to notice how quiet Mo was. For the first time in years his future seemed full of hope. He could make a real fresh start, away from all the problems, in a place where there was work, in a place where he could be alone with Mo. Away from Sheila Grant's interfering moralizing.

'If you want I could take you there tomorrow. We could see the place together. I'd go down there tonight if I could.'

Still Mo had nothing to say. Matty nudged her. 'When are we going then, girl?'

Mo took a deep breath. 'Matty, I can't go.'

'Next week then?'

'I can't go ever.'

'But I've got it all fixed.'

'We're going nowhere, Matty. This is just dreams. I want us to finish.'

Matty couldn't believe his own ears. Three days he'd been away and everything had changed. He'd gone to look

83

for a future for him and Mo. He'd planned a fresh start in a place where life was worth living. And now this. Mo saying that wasn't what she wanted. It couldn't be true. Matty felt sick with fear.

'You can't mean it. This is the best thing that's ever happened to either of us. You know that.'

'It's gone too far. I never really thought of going away.'

'You're supposed to love me, Mo, for God's sake!'

'I do. But I can't come, Matty. Not when you've left Teresa and the kids. I can't stand it on me conscience.'

'She'll be all right. I know she will.'

'She's in a terrible state.'

'What do you know about it?' Mo looked down, saying nothing. Matty thought he'd know the answer but he had to ask again. 'How d'you know that?'

'Sheila told me.'

So that was it, thought Matty. Sheila had been poking her nose in again. The interfering bitch, she'd gone too far this time. Matty's fear turned to anger. 'She's only saying that because Teresa's her mate. She wants to spoil it when for once I've found something decent, something for me.'

'She's not like that. We're finished. It's over, Matty.'

Mo turned away. Matty couldn't bear it. He tried to grab her but she shook him off. She started to run away, away from him. All Matty's happiness, all Matty's hopes were running away from him.

And it was all Sheila Grant's fault.

Matty was in despair. Then he felt murderous. This couldn't happen . . . this couldn't happen to him. He'd show Sheila. He kicked the kerb so hard his foot buckled.

'I'll kill her,' he said.

Matty had nowhere to go. Mo let him back into her house just long enough to collect a few of his things but she wouldn't listen to him when he tried to talk to her. She was cold, hard, a different woman. 'Just take what you want and go,' she said. When she closed the door behind him, Matty thought his heart would break.

84

He wouldn't go back to Teresa's. He had a pretty good idea that she would let him in and welcome him with open arms but he didn't want that. Going back to Teresa's meant admitting defeat. Worse still, it meant going back to how things had been before, and Matty couldn't bear that. He couldn't face any more days of lying in bed wondering what there was to get up for. He couldn't face seeing the kids' faces when they needed things there wasn't the money for. He couldn't face Teresa's tired patience. He couldn't face the shame of being a parasite in his own family, a man with nothing to do.

He'd tried his best to be a good husband and father, working all the hours God sent when there was work to be had. When there wasn't what place was there for him at home? That was why Mo had been important to him. She hadn't expected anything from him, she'd loved him as he was. And she had loved him. Matty remembered their time together, their nights in bed. She'd made a man of him again.

The first night after Mo left him Matty found a bed in a hostel for homeless men, but the second he couldn't bear to do even that. He slept rough under some newspaper on a bench in the park. Then, with two days' growth of beard, he went up to Brookside Close to show Sheila Grant what she had done. He pushed in the house as soon as she opened the door.

'What've you been telling Mo?'

'Matty, what's wrong?'

'You know what's wrong. Tell me why you did it.'

'I had to. For Teresa's sake.'

'You've spoilt everything. Just because you think you're better than anybody else.'

'I did it for the best.'

'You self-righteous bitch. Holier than thou!'

'I did it for the best, Matty. It would never have worked. It was a dream. You were running away from reality.'

Matty grabbed Sheila's shoulders. 'I could kill you for this.'

It was Damon, in from the garden when he heard the noise, who came to his mother's rescue. 'Don't you touch her.'

'It's between me and her. Get lost,' said Matty.

But Damon had grown up over the last few months. He was scared but firm. 'I know you're me Uncle Matty and I should respect you but I don't care. You don't touch me mum.'

'Don't talk to me like that.'

Damon stood his ground. 'Get out. I said get out.'

Matty was thunderstruck. Was this Damon, talking to him like that? The kid he'd dandled on his knee? And now Sheila was saying the same. 'Get out, Matty. Leave me alone.' Matty was at rock bottom. He had no home, nowhere to go, and now he was being thrown out of his best friend's home. 'I'll never forgive you for this,' he said to Sheila. 'You've ruined my life.'

'Just go.' Sheila was shaking.

'I'll pay you back. Just you wait.'

Sandra knew she'd let herself in for a lot of paperwork now that she had persuaded Tony to take Mr Cribbs-Baker's operating record to the GMC, and paperwork had never been her strong point. But she was committed to her case and she certainly wasn't going to let that put her off.

What she hadn't reckoned with was that Mr Cribbs-Baker knew what was going on. He stopped Tony one day as he and Sandra were going towards her car.

'May I have word, Dr Hurrell?'

Tony looked at Sandra. Mr Cribbs-Baker noticed the look without even seeming to notice that Sandra was there. 'In confidence, of course.'

'I'm sure Sister Maghie will respect any confidence.'

'I'd rather not,' said Cribbs-Baker, and then to Sandra: 'I'm sure you understand, dear.'

86

Sandra had no choice but to get into the car and sit fuming as they walked away. Mr Cribbs-Baker's attitude to women was summed up in the way he'd spoken to her. 'Dear' indeed, as if she were a child to be patronized. But that was how he always was. Smooth, conciliatory, ever so kind but always in a totally patronizing way. As if no one who was female could possibly have a brain in her head or a mind of her own. And he treated women's bodies just as dismissively. Sandra dreaded to think what he might be saying to Tony.

Her dread was well founded. Cribbs-Baker came straight to the point. 'I believe you have plans to take charges against me to the GMC. You and the popsy.'

'So?'

'Let me tell you now you'll be wasting your time.'

'We think we have evidence to prove that several of your operations were unnecessary.'

Cribbs-Baker's manner became a little less bland. 'You do realize that if I had a witness to what you've just said . . . unnecessary operations . . . I could sue?'

'We've got a case and we want to present it.'

'And that's worth more to you than your career?'

'Is that a threat?'

'Let's call it good sense shall we? If you carry on like this you'll find doors slammed in your face all over the place. Would any consultant want a zealous young doctor watching his every move?'

Tony was horribly afraid that he was right. The fact was that any future progress he made in the profession that was his life depended on the approval of people like Cribbs-Baker. They had the power, and they'd support one another. Was it worth taking matters any further?

Cribbs-Baker knew he was winning. He pressed his advantage. 'Look here old chap, you're obviously not an advocate of good old-fashioned skills like the knife. Why not try for a position where they go more for thera-peutics?' And as Tony was still silent, 'I have friends who can open doors. Need I say more?'

Not thinking, Tony blurted out what was on his mind. 'What about Sandra?' Mr Cribbs-Baker smiled the smile of a man who has won. 'Word is spreading about her part in this. This business won't have done her career any good at all.'

From the way Tony walked back to the car Sandra had a good idea what had happened. Still, she listened whilst he told her and as he did so her indignation mounted.

'It's blackmail.'

'We can't prove it.'

'I know what's happened. He has a word in your ear and after five minutes, you cave in.' Tony was silent, agreeing. Sandra couldn't stop. 'Stick together, don't you? I dare say he told you he could help your career.'

'It's our word against his. And he's got the clout.'

Sandra banged the pile of papers. 'We've got evidence. Look at all this.'

'Doctors have different opinions.'

'You're looking after your career, aren't you? Why risk money for a few women?'

Tony was stung. 'It's not the money. I want to be a doctor . . . I've always wanted it. There's things I can do in medicine and I'm not chucking that away.'

Distress made Sandra shout. 'All this work . . . all this . . . and you throw it away at one word from him. Well he'll not beat me so easily.'

'Go easy, Sandra. You'll not do yourself any good.'

'Threatened me too, did he?'

'Yes.'

'Well, I don't care.'

Tony sat silent. Sandra knew she'd lost. If she was going to do anything more she'd be on her own.

She devoted her next day off to that task. The only way forward now was through the press. Pat came in to find her making a selection of what papers to send.

'I thought you'd given that up?'

'Not when women's futures are at stake.'

Pat sighed. They seemed to have been here before. 'You're risking your career.'

This was near enough the truth to hurt. 'Don't try and stop me from doing what I think is right.'

'I want to stop you making a fool of yourself. That evidence won't stand up.'

'There's six cases here that could have been treated by chemo-therapy or laser. Women . . . young women . . . who've lost their wombs for no reason except to line someone's pocket. Mr Cribbs-Baker's pocket. It's in the case notes, the biopsy showed nothing wrong.'

'Everything you have is a matter of professional interpretation. And I know why you're doing this.'

'Oh yes?'

'His name's Tony Hurrell. *Doctor* Tony Hurrell.'

'Can't you leave Tony out of it?'

Pat's jealousy boiled up. 'No I can't. Hasn't he been practically living in this house for weeks?'

'Not that again.'

'Yeah, that again.' Suddenly Pat lost all control. 'I'm not daft you know, I'm not stupid. I know you're having an affair with him.'

Sandra hadn't seen Tony for two days but she certainly wasn't going to let Pat know that. 'That's all in your mind.'

'Well, if it's not him, who is it?'

'How dare you!' Sandra leapt up, facing Pat.

'It must be somebody because it's certainly not me. You've not let me near you for weeks.'

'Why should I? You've done nothing but get at me. What help have I had from you over this?'

'Why should I help you make a fool of yourself? I'll tell you what's really going on. Tony Hurrell's trying to get rid of Cribbs-Baker so he can have his job. And you're daft enough to help him.'

'Oh you . . . you . . .' Speechless with rage Sandra pushed at Pat. He pushed her away so she nearly fell, and then, leaning forward, swept all her papers on to the floor. She stood up, shaking. 'That's it. You've gone too far.'

Pat, chastened, went towards her. 'San, I'm sorry . . . I didn't mean . . .' But it was too late. Sandra raised her hand and clawed at his face.

Pat raised his hand in return. Then, seeing the look on Sandra's face, he dropped it. There was only one way to make sure he wouldn't do something he would always regret and that was to put a lot of distance between himself and Sandra until he cooled down. Desperately Pat rushed for the door. He had to get as far away as possible for as long as possible. The van was outside. The keys were still in the door.

Pat didn't care what he did. He was exceeding the speed limit even before he got to the end of the Close.

Chapter Seven

Harry Cross was inspecting his car slowly, very slowly indeed. He wasn't really looking at anything very much because all his energies were concentrated on listening to his neighbours. Despite his age Harry's hearing was good, and in the summer, when people left their windows open there was plenty to listen to. So he couldn't help hearing Pat and Sandra's row, and he wasn't surprised when Pat rushed out and drove like a madman out of the Close.

The row at the Grants' was more muted, but it was a row nonetheless.

'You're meeting who?' asked Bobby incredulously.

Sheila sighed. 'You heard.'

'Yes, but I don't believe it. I never thought I'd live to see this.'

'Live to see what?'

'My wife meeting another fellow. In a pub.'

'There's no need to put it like that. All I said was that I'm going to meet Alun Jones to discuss going further with my education. I'm meeting him because he's my tutor, there's nothing more to it than that.'

'That's sheer hypocrisy. You break up Matty and Mo and then you go off with this bloke.'

'I'm not going off with him. It's to discuss education, that's all . . . Come with us if you want.'

Bobby wasn't mollified. 'No chance! That'd really spoil things, wouldn't it?'

'The offer's there. If you think you can behave yourself, come. If not, stop at home.'

Bobby didn't offer Sheila a lift after that, and she wouldn't have accepted if he had. She caught the bus to meet Alun. Sheila hated falling out with Bobby and the quarrel had cast a blight over the evening, but she was determined to go out nevertheless. Alun was right, it was time she did something for herself.

Alun got the drinks in, and then settled down to business. 'You mustn't stop now you know. You've got the potential to go much further than this simple little course.'

'It may be simple for you but I find it pretty hard work.'

'You're not in the habit of study yet. You soon would be on a full-time course.'

'What about our Claire? She's not two yet.'

'You could make arrangements. Don't close your mind to it.'

Sheila didn't want to. She felt like a new woman since she'd started thinking and reading. Her brain seemed to have woken up. She read the paper more thoroughly now, and had begun to see how what happened in London or in other parts of the world affected people in Liverpool. For the first time in her life, Sheila felt she had some grasp of what was going on, instead of simply being at the mercy of events. She'd very much like to carry on learning more.

But Bobby didn't like the idea. He was anxious about the changes that might mean.

'Funny things happen on courses, don't they?' Sheila said. 'People change. Look at Matty.'

'What about Matty?'

'Well . . . him and Mo. It really turned his life upside down, coming on this course.'

'Perhaps it was time.'

'What do you mean?'

'People move on. Perhaps it was time for Matty to look for something new.'

'Something new! You make it sound like a new toy. It's not just something new for Matty, it's a person. People's lives are affected. Look at Teresa.'

'It could be best for her too, once she's got over the shock,' Alun said. 'She could make a fresh start too . . . lots of women do.'

Sheila's Catholic conscience spoke. 'Marriage is for ever.'

'Not always. Why should people stay together if it stops them progressing? Matty has a future with Mo, a fresh start with a woman who understood him. You've seen the change in him. He's a new man. Mo's made him happy.'

'But Matty and Teresa were happy.'

'Were they? Both of them?'

This struck home. Sheila remembered Matty's despair over the last months when he'd realized he'd never work again. He'd thought of moving then, away from Liverpool, finding somewhere to begin again. But Teresa wouldn't leave her mother and sisters. 'What'll I do,' she'd said. 'I won't know anybody?'

'There's people everywhere,' Matty had said. 'You'll get to know them.' But Teresa wasn't having any, and Matty had given up the idea, and with it his last vestiges of fighting spirit. He'd seemed like a beaten man after that, taking no interest in life, letting himself go. Until he'd met Mo. What was it he'd said? 'Mo's given me hope. She means a fresh start.' Maybe it wasn't as simple as Sheila had thought.

Alun was carrying on with his theme. 'People do grow out of people you know. 'Specially if one of them's brighter than the other.' Sheila began to feel uncomfortable. She knew what he was getting at: her and Bob. Alun moved his leg nearer to Sheila's. 'I've been married as well you know. I know about putting up with someone just because you are married to them. Is that good enough?'

Sheila definitely didn't want this. Firmly she turned the conversation. 'I've come to talk about my education. Where can I go from here?'

Bobby was sitting at home on his own and not liking it.

He even wished Claire would wake up. At least she would be a bit of company and take his mind off his thoughts. It couldn't really be true that Sheila fancied this fellow, could it? What was it she'd said to him once, when he'd jibbed at her going on an overnight course. 'What you don't like is that I won't be here to wait on you. I'm just going to learn, that's all. It's not all like *Educating Rita* you know.'

Bobby wasn't so sure of that. Sheila wasn't worldly-wise, she thought everybody was like her, still doing what the priest said. Bobby had seen the way Alun Jones looked at Sheila and he didn't trust him, didn't trust him an inch.

His musing was interrupted by a banging on the front door. That'd be Karen or Damon forgetting their key again, thought Bobby. Heads like sieves the pair of them. Irritated, he got to his feet.

But it wasn't either Karen or Damon. It was Sally Dinsdale, Sheila's friend from the class. Bobby hadn't seen her since the night she'd moved into the hostel for battered wives. She looked a lot better this time.

Bobby peered past her, looking for the children. She realized what he wanted. 'I've left them at the hostel, one of the other women is looking after them. I just wanted a word with Sheila.'

'She's not in, love.'

Sally was disappointed. 'Will she be long?'

Bobby just stopped himself saying, 'She'd better not be,' and said instead, 'Shouldn't be. D'you want to come in and wait?'

Whilst Bobby was making a cup of coffee, Sally told him why she'd come. 'It's Ken. We've had a row.'

'I thought he didn't know where you were?' Bobby couldn't resist being sarcastic. 'I thought this hostel place was supposed to be secret from all men, even me.'

'Supposed to be, yeah, but he's found out. Luckily the women wouldn't let him in so he didn't get near the kids.'

'He got near you?'

Sally looked uncomfortable. 'Shouldn't have let him really, should I? At least that's what the women said. But he looked so pathetic I just went out to have a word.'

Bobby hardly thought of Ken Dinsdale as pathetic, remembering some of the dreadful injuries he'd seen on Sally. But then he must look different to Sally or she would never have stayed with him for so long.

'I came to warn Sheila,' said Sally. 'He blames her for what's happened.'

He might be right, thought Bobby, but had the sense not to say it. How many times had he told Sheila that it would only cause trouble if she kept on poking her nose into other people's business?

Talking about Ken was making Sally get upset. 'Ken's been drinking all day, you see. And you know how that affects him.' Bobby did indeed. It was when he'd been drinking that Ken Dinsdale got violent and attacked his wife.

'I wonder you weren't afraid to talk to him.'

'I wouldn't have if I'd known. But he seemed sober when I agreed. I didn't know he had a bottle with him. Besides, it's not me he wants to get at today. It's Sheila. He blames her for persuading me to leave. Said I never would if she hadn't helped.'

Bobby was anxious. 'D'you think he'll go looking for her?'

'He won't know where she is. He only knows the class and here.'

'Well, she's not at the class.'

'That's all right then.' Sally went on to wax lyrical about Sheila. 'I don't know what I would have done without her these last few months, she's been such a help to me.'

Instead of to her own family, thought Bobby, but again said nothing.

'You must be so proud of her since she started this course,' said Sally. 'She's doing better than any of us.'

'She seems to enjoy it right enough.'

'Alun reckons she might even go to university eventually. She's the best in the class, you know.'

'I know about me own wife.'

'Of course Alun thinks the sun shines out of her. She's really teacher's pet.'

'Is she?'

'Oh yes. But then she deserves to be, doesn't she?'

'Hmm.'

When he'd shown Sally out Bobby wondered if he should go and look for Sheila just to be on the safe side. But then, how could he? He imagined what she'd say if he walked into the pub and found her with Alun. Worse, he imagined the look on Alun's face. She'd already refused his offer to pick her up at nine o'clock. 'Stop fussing, will you,' she'd said irritably. 'I'm a big girl you know, I can look after myself. Anyway Alun's got a car. He'll give me a lift home.'

Teacher's pet indeed.

Over Sheila's second drink of the evening and his fourth, Alun raised the matter of the weekend school again.

'It'd do a lot for you, Sheila. You'd be amazed what you can learn on an intensive weekend like that.'

'I've said no, haven't I?'

'But why? You'd really enjoy it. And it'd do you good to get away.'

'I can't, not just at the minute. Bob's been having a hard time at work.'

'That's it, is it? Bob again, standing in your way.'

'It's not like that.'

'Yes it is, admit it. The sky's the limit if only he'd give you a chance. And we could get to know each other so much better on a weekend.'

Sheila tried to take the heat out of the situation with humour. 'We know each other already, don't we? What sort of a woman would I be, sitting here with you if we didn't?'

96

'You're a wonderful woman, Sheila. And I want to get to know you better, much better. It's difficult at the class isn't it, there's always someone else? But on this weekend we'd be alone together, just the two of us.'

Sheila was feeling very uncomfortable now. She shifted further up the seat away from Alun. She tried to find words to say no without causing offence.

'I'm sure it would be nice, Alun, but I can't. I'm a married woman, I've got a family. They need looking after.'

'You would like to though?'

'Well yes. If I could.' For a moment Sheila was tempted. It would be nice to go away, have a whole weekend to think and talk and learn. But it wasn't possible. 'It isn't that I don't want to,' she said, 'but I can't.'

'If only . . .' said Alun, and put his hand over hers.

Karen came in from a night out with Guy, to find her father on his own staring at the television.

'Sorry I'm late, but me and Guy have been planning what to do during the summer holidays.'

'Oh.'

'Anything the matter, dad?'

'No. Why should there be?'

Karen gave up and went upstairs to find Damon.

'What's the matter with dad?'

'Mum's out.'

'I can see that. But why does that make him so narky?'

'She's with that Alun Jones.'

'Oh I see. Talking about the course?'

'He thinks that fellow's after her.'

'Our mum? Don't be daft. I dunno, men, they're all the same, only thinking of one thing. Women have got minds as well as bodies you know.'

'Tell dad that.'

But when Karen heard from Bobby about Sally's visit she too began to be anxious. 'You don't think mum's in any danger, do you?'

'If I did for a second I wouldn't be here,' said Bobby.

'Shouldn't you go down to the pub and get her home?'

'She'd only think we were spying on her.'

'Well it's up to you, I suppose.'

In the pub Sheila was still anxious to get away from Alun. But her firm reply seemed to have cooled him down for the moment and besides she was stuck in the corner and it would be very obvious if she tried to push her way out. More than that, she had no intention of going home whilst things were awkward. That would just prove Bobby right all along. Sheila decided to work on getting back on an even keel with Alun so that she could leave with dignity, making it clear she liked him just as a friend.

Then things went very badly wrong. She suddenly became aware of someone standing, staring at her. She looked up from her glass of shandy. It was Matty.

He looked terrible, much worse than when she'd last seen him. It was obvious he'd gone on sleeping rough and lost any pride in his appearance. Even worse were his eyes. They were full of hate.

There was what seemed an endless silence. Then Matty spoke, not bothering to lower his voice. 'It's you, is it? You hypocritical bitch.'

'Not in here, Matty, please.'

'Why not? Where else is there to go? I've been sleeping in the gutter because of you.'

Alun tried to defend Sheila. 'Leave her alone.'

'Leave her to you, you mean.' Matty turned to Sheila again. 'You're nothing but a moralizing liar. You tell lies to Mo, split us up, and what do you do? Meet your fancy man in the pub.'

'Now wait a minute.' Alun stood up and might have gone for Matty but Sheila held him back.

'It's not like that,' she said.

'Isn't it? Didn't I see him hold your hand. Very cosy.'

98

He turned to Alun. 'Hasn't she told you that it's a terrible sin to carry on with a married woman? Or doesn't it apply to you and her?'

Sheila had to stop this. 'Matty, stop making a fool of yourself.'

'I'm not making a fool of myself. Not as much as I did all those years I thought you were my friend.' He raised his voice so the pub could hear. 'See this one here? She goes round splitting other people up, but all the time she's carrying on with the teacher.'

Sheila was really distressed now. 'We're not carrying on.'

Alun looked at her. 'That's not exactly true, Sheila.'

Sheila was desperate. 'What are you saying, Alun?'

'You know there's something between us. Don't deny me, I can't bear it. You wanted to come away with me, you said so yourself.'

Matty gloated. 'Planning a dirty weekend were you?'

'No,' said Sheila.

'Not a dirty weekend. A wonderful weekend,' said Alun.

Sheila felt trapped. There they were, two against one. Men, bigger than her, and with louder voices, saying what she knew wasn't true, and with the whole room listening. She no longer cared about politeness or even decency. She had to get away from here, she had to get home.

Desperately she pushed past Alun, tipping the table till the glasses fell on the floor. Heedless of staring faces she ran for the door. She just had to get out.

A taxi had just drawn up outside. Sheila grabbed at it, hanging on to the door as if to make sure it didn't get away. The time it took for the passengers to get out seemed interminable.

Matty and Alun had followed her out, one threatening, the other begging.

'You don't get away like that,' Matty said.

Alun tried to hold her arm. 'Say you care for me. We were planning to go away.'

Sheila shook herself free. 'Alun, I don't know how you got that idea . . .'

'Idea! It wasn't an idea. We were talking about it.'

The taxi driver pocketed his fare and revved his engine. 'You coming or what?' he said to Sheila.

'Wait.' Quickly Sheila jumped in. 'Brookside Close, please.'

The cabbie had heard what was going on. 'Not taking the boyfriend?'

'He's not my boyfriend. Please take me home.' As the car started, Alun banged on the door. 'Don't do this to me.' Horrified, Sheila heard his feet thud against the car door. Behind her, on the other side of the cab, Matty flung himself in and on to the seat beside her. 'Oh no you don't. You don't get away as easy as that,' he said.

'Matty, please go away.' The taxi had gathered speed now.

'No. I'm going to haunt you everywhere you go.'

This wasn't the Matty Sheila knew. 'Don't talk like that. You don't know what you're doing. You've been drinking.'

'Why shouldn't I? What else is there to do?'

'Listen to me . . .'

'Listen! That's what Mo did, and then look what happened. I'll not listen to you, it's your turn to listen to me.'

He grasped her arm hard, so hard that it hurt. Sheila could stand no more. She banged on the driver's shoulder. 'Stop please. Stop here.' The cabbie turned. 'You sure? It's miles away from anywhere.' Outside there was nothing but a patch of wasteland and some trees but Sheila didn't care. She had to get out of the car and away from Matty.

'This'll do. Just put me down.'

The cabbie shrugged and put his foot on the brake. 'Up to you.'

Sheila got out and thrust some coins through the window. 'Here you are. Just leave me.'

The driver took the money and shrugged. 'Suit yourself lady. Rather you than me.'

The taxi drove off, Matty with it. Sheila was alone.

Tears rose, and then great sobs, shaking her whole body. How had things come to this? How could this be happening to her? All she'd done was try to help Teresa, try to better herself, and now here she was alone and frightened. She didn't deserve it. Now she was away from all the shouting, all the blame, her legs turned to jelly. Shaking all over she sat down by the side of the road.

Inside the taxi it was Matty's turn to bang on the driver's shoulder.

'Drop me off here, mate.'

'Here? We've only gone a few hundred yards.'

'You heard what I said. No point going any further. I couldn't pay you anyway.'

'Well in that case . . .' The driver stopped. 'What about what's up on my clock?'

'Sheila gave you plenty.' Matty climbed out and banged the door of the cab after him. 'If it's any more send the bill to her. Sheila Grant, 5 Brookside Close.'

Sheila was still sitting by the side of the road. She was calmer now, but still weeping. The shock of the last hour had begun to catch up with her. How was she going to get home?

Behind her she heard footsteps. A man's voice called her name.

'Sheila.'

Who was it? Sheila half turned to see and caught a glimpse of a man's dark silhouette but she couldn't make out his features. He was coming towards her fast. She tried to get up but before she could gather the strength something dark and stifling covered her head. She struggled, panicking. What was this?

She struggled more desperately but couldn't get free. The man was bigger and stronger than her, his arms were round her now and he was dragging her away from the road.

Sheila's heart raced. She tried to call for help but no sound came. Then she was pushed to the ground and hands pulled at her clothes, touched her body. There was no escape. This was real, it was really happening. To her.

Bobby, sitting at home, was getting angrier and angrier. He walked to the window, looked at his watch, and looked through the window again. Karen could stand it no longer.

'Why don't you go and get her?'

'Nine o'clock she said she'd be in. Look at the time now.' It was half past nine.

'Why don't you just go for her, dad?'

'Like she said, she's grown-up. Up to her when she comes in.'

'But she's late, isn't she? That's not like mum.'

'Not like she used to be, you mean.'

'I think we should go,' said Karen. 'I'll come with you. Our Damon'll baby-sit, won't you?'

'I was just going to go . . .' said Damon.

Karen nodded towards the agitated Bobby. 'Just do it,' she said.

Bobby had got his coat. 'I'll go on me own. I can sort it out. No need for anybody else.'

'I'm coming,' said Karen, unexpectedly firm. 'The mood you're in you'll probably belt Alun Jones if somebody's not there to stop you.'

Bobby went towards the door. 'I don't know what all the fuss is about.'

Karen looked at Damon as she went out. 'Don't you?' she said. 'You should try listening to yourself.'

Sheila didn't know how long she lay on the ground after the man had finished with her. He whipped his coat away as he went but she couldn't lift her head to look. She felt frightened, dirty, and quite unbearably humiliated. She pulled her clothes down and covered her face with her arms. She didn't want to look or be looked at.

Bit by bit she collected her thoughts. She was shivering with cold and fright. Cautiously she moved. No bones broken, she thought. The memory of the familiar phrase brought the relief of tears. It was what her mother used to say when they were children: '. . . Lets have a look, love . . . well, no bones broken.' Then, it had meant that no real harm was done. Now, broken bones or not, harm had been done. Sheila felt damaged, damaged beyond repair. Suddenly she wanted to be at home. In her room, alone, safe behind locked doors. On the road a hundred yards away Karen and Bobby drove past. Just too late, Sheila began to get to her feet.

When there was no sign of Sheila at the pub, Bobby's face darkened. 'If she's not here, where is she?' he demanded.

Karen thought fast. 'Maybe she went to see Sally.'

'And maybe she didn't.'

'It could be anything, dad.'

'That's what I'm afraid of.' They walked back to the car in a brooding silence.

Sheila never knew how she got home. She just walked, putting one foot after the other in a daze, finding her way by instinct, not thinking . . . not thinking about anything. At the house Damon was alone, glued to the television. She walked past the back of him, not speaking. 'Hi mum,' he said, seeing only her back as she went upstairs.

In the bathroom she locked the door and filled the bath full of water as hot as she could bear. It was so hot it hurt Sheila as she climbed in but she didn't mind. The hotter it was the cleaner she would get. She picked up the soap and started to scrub herself. If only she could wash her thoughts away.

When she'd finished she wrapped herself in a dressing gown and knelt by the side of the bath, dropping her clothes into the still-steaming water. Downstairs, Bobby had come home.

'Mum's in,' said Damon.

Bobby was still angry. 'Where?'

'She went upstairs.'

Bobby ran up the stairs and stood outside the bathroom door.

'Are you there, Sheila?'

Sheila dropped more clothes into the bath water. Then she poured disinfectant after them. She was sobbing quietly, hopelessly. Bobby shouted again. 'Open up, Shei. Let me in.'

Sheila dropped the last of her clothes in the bath. Bobby was getting angrier now. He hammered on the door. 'What you playing at? Let me in will ya? I want to know what's been going on.' Sheila stood, her hand on the bolt, tears streaming, afraid to go out. Bobby lost patience. 'Come out and face me, can't you? Or don't you dare? Have you been with him?' He aimed a kick at the door. 'D'you want me to kick it down?'

Sheila took a deep breath and slowly opened the door. She just stood there. Bobby fell silent. One look at her face was enough to tell him that something was wrong. Very wrong.

'What is it, Shei? What's happened?' He put his hand out to touch Sheila but she jerked back. Bobby was gentle now. 'For God's sake, tell me what's the matter.'

At last Sheila found words. 'There was a man . . . I've been attacked.' She leaned against the wall, shaking, struggling to get the word out. 'Raped.'

Bobby's first thought was to destroy whoever had done it: hurt them as they'd hurt Sheila. His second was to hold Sheila and never let her go again. His third, the worst, was to hate himself. She'd been through that, and what had he done? Shouted at her, accused her, banged the door. 'I'm sorry,' he said. 'I'm sorry . . . I'm sorry . . .'

Wearily, Sheila shook her head. 'Don't . . . don't go on. Don't say anything. Just let me be.'

★

George William's timing couldn't have been worse. He knocked on the front door just as Bobby and Karen had got Sheila into bed. Damon went to answer the knock and stared unseeingly at George as he asked if Bobby was in. George had to repeat the question twice before he recovered enough to let him in.

It was impossible to conceal what had happened from George. None of them were in any state to put on a brave face. George sat with his coat still on, scarcely able to look Bobby in the face. 'Jeeze, Bob. I don't know what to say.'

'Nothing anybody can say.'

'If there's anything I can do . . .'

If only anybody could, thought Bobby. It was a kind thought, but the best thing George could do would be to leave them alone. 'You didn't say why you came?' he said. George thought furiously. He'd come to tell Bobby the result of the NEC meeting, that he was suspended for a month. But this didn't seem the time for bad news. 'Oh . . . just bits and pieces . . . really I was just wanting to keep you in the picture. But under the circumstances . . .' Inspiration struck. 'Tell you what,' said George, 'why don't you just take compassionate leave. I'll not want to see you in the office for a month.'

For a long time after she was put to bed with a hot water bottle, Sheila just lay, staring at the ceiling, unwilling to close her eyes. At first she didn't want anybody near her, she wouldn't even let Bobby hold her hand. There was nothing he could do but sit there, watching her. But gradually she stopped shaking and relaxed. After a while, she seemed to doze, and Bobby crept downstairs. He went towards the telephone.

'What you doing?' asked Karen.

'Calling the police. What d'you think?'

'Don't,' said Karen. 'Leave her till morning.'

Bobby was appalled. 'I can't do that. She's been attacked. We've got to get the fellow who did it.'

Karen was insistent. 'She needs quiet.'

Damon supported his father. 'We've got to get this fellow.'

'D'you realize what it'll involve?' said Karen.

'What?' asked Damon.

Karen had to spell it out. 'They'll take her through it. Every detail. She'll have to talk about it. It'll be like . . . like being raped again.'

Bobby was horrified. 'She couldn't stand that.'

'And it's not just the questions,' said Karen. 'They'll have to check for bruises . . . take swabs. It's too soon.'

And Bobby, remembering Sheila's face, had to agree. He'd leave it for now. But only for now. They had to find who did it. And when they did . . . The way Bobby felt, whoever it was wouldn't live to tell the tale.

Chapter Eight

Neither Shelia nor Bobby got much sleep that night. Every time Sheila closed her eyes she was haunted by images of what had happened . . . and what might have happened. She could only keep them away by staying awake. She kept a lamp lit so that she could see where she was. This was her room, this was her bed. This man was her husband. But she lay stiff and rigid and as far away from him as possible. She couldn't bear anyone to touch her, not even Bobby. And all the time there were the questions. Why had she gone out? Why had she got out of the taxi? What had she done to deserve this?

For Bobby there was only one question: Who?

Next door but one, Sandra was sleepless too. After the scene with Pat she had made her decision: the relationship with him was definitely at an end. With Terry's help she had moved all her things across to Kate's bedroom. This time, memories or not, she was determined to stay.

She lay for a long time listening for the sound of Pat's key in the lock. She wasn't exactly worried about him. After his attempt to hit her she had finally lost all feeling for him, she'd had too much violence in her marriage to risk a repeat. But she couldn't help wondering where he was. The mood he was in anything could have happened.

In fact there was no chance of Pat getting home that night. He was in no position to go anywhere. If he'd tried, several large policemen were on hand to stop him. He'd been picked up by the police at about ten o'clock that night, he couldn't remember why or where. All he knew was that he wished they'd let him lie down and sleep.

A constable stood impassively by the interview room door as Detective Sergeant Whalley grilled Pat. 'What you been up to then?'

'I dunno.' Pat tried to shake his head to reinforce the negative but at each shake his head banged as if his brains were loose in his skull. He remembered a row with Sandra and then going in a pub, or maybe two, and buying a bottle of vodka. After that, nothing. 'I want out of here,' he said. 'I haven't done anything.'

Whalley wasn't convinced. 'Oh no? You weren't keen on talking to us were you? The minute you spotted our patrol car you ran for it. Why?'

What patrol car? Pat tried shaking his head to clear it but again it made things worse. 'I dunno. I feel sick.'

'When you're really sick, we'll get you a bucket. Now what you been up to? People don't run for no reason.'

Pat tried to concentrate. Something came back. 'I was driving the van . . .'

'What van? There was no van. We didn't see one.'

'Oh.' Pat rubbed his face.

Whalley leaned forward and pulled his hand away. 'You don't hide them that easy.'

'Hide what?'

'The scratches. On your face.'

Vaguely somewhere in the battlefield that was his head, Pat remembered something. A fight. Scratches. Oh God . . . He let his head fall on his hands. 'What's she going to say now?' he said. 'She'll never let me near again.'

Whalley leaned forward. 'She . . . a woman? Who?' But Pat was past thinking any more. He just wanted to be left alone. 'I dunno,' he said. 'I don't know anything.'

Abruptly Whalley stood up and spoke to the constable. 'Find out what's happened tonight will you? Anything that's happened within a thousand miles of where he was picked up . . . anything . . . I want to know about it.'

*

Nobody at the Grants' felt any better the next morning. But for Bobby, the next step was clear. He sat at the side of the bed talking to Sheila gently but urgently.

'We've got to do something, love. Let me call the police.'

'No.' Sheila said. She never wanted to see anybody again, let alone strangers. Certainly not the police.

Bobby didn't give up. 'You wouldn't wish this on any other poor girl, would you?' Sheila thought of Karen. 'No . . .'

'Then we've got to report it, Shei. We've got to help catch him.'

'I'm scared. I don't want to talk about it.'

Bobby touched her hand and this time she didn't draw back. 'I'll be with you,' he said.

'I don't feel like going out. I couldn't face it.'

'They'll come here. Honest they will. I'll see to that. We've got to stop him doing this again.'

Sheila remembered, and then tried to forget. Yes, they'd got to stop him doing that to someone else. 'All right,' she said.

'Good.'

'D'you think they'll blame me for what happened?'

'No. Why should they?'

'I don't know.'

But Sheila couldn't help feeling guilty. Perhaps she had done something wrong. Perhaps she'd led Alun on, though she'd never meant to. Perhaps just by being out, just by being a woman, she'd asked for what had happened. Hadn't her mother always warned her to be careful where she went and what she wore and who she talked to?

The police sent two officers, both in plain clothes. The woman, Detective Sergeant Spencer, went up to Sheila's bedroom. She was a kind but insistent interviewer, jogging Sheila's memory when the last thing Sheila wanted to do was remember.

'Did he say anything to you?'

'No. Only my name.'

Sergeant Spencer wrote that down. 'Anything else? Anything obscene?' Then, as Sheila was silent, 'You can tell me. We've heard it all before you know.'

'No. Nothing.'

'Any identifying marks? Anything at all you can remember?'

'I didn't see him. There was this thing you see. Over my head. I thought I'd suffocate.'

'So you wouldn't recognize him again?'

'Only . . . the smell.'

'What about it?'

'Him. Sweat and dirt.' Sheila wanted to vomit but her stomach was empty.

'And this was last night around nine o'clock?'

'Yes.'

'So why didn't you report it yesterday?'

Sheila just looked. Had this woman any idea of how she felt?

'A lot of these attacks you see, they're by men known to the woman,' said Spencer. 'That's why they're not reported. I have to ask this, Mrs Grant, have you got a relationship with a man other than your husband?'

Sheila's mind suddenly started to function. She knew, clear as a bell, what this was getting at. Anger gave her the courage to speak out.

'You mean was I having an affair? Am I making this up in case my husband finds out?'

'You did say you were meeting this tutor . . . Mr Jones.'

Sheila felt helpless. They were blaming her. 'Yes, but that was only about the class . . .' Sheila's voice faded. Would this woman believe her?

'We have to ask.'

Wearily Sheila started to cry. 'D'you think I'd go through this if it wasn't true? I wish it wasn't true, but it really happened.'

*

Downstairs, Bobby was telling Det. Constable Bryant everything he knew. About Sheila meeting Alun in the pub, about the anonymous letter Sheila had received, about Sally going to the hostel and Ken Dinsdale's reaction.

'He threatened your wife?'

'At the night school, yes. There are witnesses.'

Damon joined in. He'd known all along who he'd put his money on. 'He did more than just threaten. He was watching her. In his car at the end of the Close.'

Bobby turned on Damon. 'Why didn't you tell me?'

'You were away. In London.'

'Why didn't she tell me?'

'She knew you'd go mad.'

'I should never have gone to London.'

'What kind of man is he?' asked Bryant. 'Is he the violent type?'

'I'd say so. He's violent to his own wife. I've seen the bruises.'

Sergeant Spencer came out of Sheila's bedroom and called downstairs. 'Pete.'

' 'Scuse me a minute,' said Bryant and went upstairs. They met on the landing. 'How's it going?' Bryant asked.

'She seems genuine. What about the husband?'

'He had the girl with him all the time. He's not got a lot of good to say about this tutor bloke.'

'D'you think that's who it is?'

'Maybe. There's someone else who's worth following up . . . Ken Dinsdale.'

'She had a row with a fellow in the pub. Name of Matty Nolan, someone she knew before. She's not saying much, but that's why she left.'

'Plenty to follow up.'

'Well, it's the real thing so we'd better get on with it. You call through to the station. I'll get her to come down there for the examination.'

'What about her clothes?'

'They'll not be much help. In the bath water all night. She bathed herself as well.'

'I only wish people would realize that's destroying evidence.'

'I don't think thinking ahead was top of her priorities last night. She was upset, Pete. Most women just want to get clean. I can understand it, but it doesn't help us.'

On his way downstairs, Bryant caught Karen's eye. He realized from her face she'd been listening. 'You shouldn't be there,' he said.

'I've a right to know what's going on. At least I believe my mum. Do you?'

'I do now.'

'Because your mate says so?'

'We have to check it out.'

'You can't not believe her.'

'It's not as easy as that. We have to be sure. She might have to stand up in court.'

Bobby was horrified. 'Oh no, not that. Will she have to say it again . . . all this . . . in public?'

'If we catch him. You want him caught, don't you?'

And there was nothing more they could say.

Only steely determination not to break down got Sheila through the physical examination. The doctor who did the tests was kind, but he was another stranger intruding when she most wanted to be left alone. She did what she was told like a zombie, supported only by Bobby's conviction that it was the right thing to do.

If only she'd seen who it was. If only she knew. But she hadn't seen, and she didn't know, and the man was still free somewhere out there. Knowing. Waiting.

When the report of Sheila's attack came in, it didn't help Pat one bit. It didn't take Whalley long to connect the two addresses and then he was back again with his questions. 'How d'you get on with your neighbours? Women neighbours?'

'What's my neighbours to do with me being here?'

'Don't ask questions, just answer them. These neighbours . . . who d'you get on with best?'

'Sheila, I suppose.'

'Oh yes?'

'She's very nice.'

'I see. Know her well, do you? Like her a lot?'

'What's this about?'

'Does her old man know you two get on well?'

'For God's sake she's a friend, that's all. I talk to her when I've got problems.'

'Got any problems at the moment?'

Pat thought of Sandra. 'Yes.'

'Well, you might be interested to know a woman was attacked last night.'

'What's that to do with me?'

'We don't know yet, do we? But we'll find out. We'll find out what you were doing. How you got those scratches on your face.'

When it seemed there was nothing more he could do to help, Damon decided he'd be best out of the way. He went across to see Sandra.

'Remember you asked if I'd do some decorating for you?'

'Aye.'

'When d'you want me to start? Any time'd suit me.'

'Now?'

'Yes, please.'

'Start on Kate's room . . . my room. I'd like it done as soon as possible. I want it clean . . . different.'

Damon was on his way upstairs with some pots of paint, when the phone rang. Terry answered, and called for Sandra. 'It's Pat. He wants to speak to you.'

'I'm not coming. If he can't be bothered coming home all night I'm not talking to him.'

'He's in a right state.' Terry listened to the phone and

then called more urgently, 'You'll have to come, Sand . . . He says the police have got him.'

Sandra came reluctantly. It was clear she had no intention of forgetting what had happened or forgiving Pat.

Damon hung about on the stairs, pretending to tie his shoe-lace, trying to find out what was going on.

'What's he done?' asked Terry when Sandra put the phone down. 'What's he in the cop shop for?'

'They picked him up last night. He was plastered.'

'What about the van?' asked Terry.' I hope he's not crashed it. We're supposed to be out on a job this morning.'

'He doesn't know where the van is. That's one of the things they keep asking him. He doesn't remember much about anything.'

'What they got him for? Drunk and disorderly?'

'More than that. They're questioning him over an assault on a woman.'

'Pat? Never! He's not violent.'

'Oh no?' said Sandra flatly. 'So what d'you call what happened here last night?'

'Well . . . he's got a temper. But why should he attack a stranger?'

'This is worse than an attack. It's a rape.'

Damon shot downstairs. 'Who? Where?'

'What's it to you?' Terry asked.

'My mum . . .' began Damon, and then realized he'd given the game away. He put the paint pots down. He'd lost heart for the decorating now. 'D'you mind if I leave it? Just for now.'

But when he got home Damon wasn't sure what to say. He hung around, getting in the way until Bobby lost his temper.

'For goodness sake, lad, stop mooching around. Can't you see your mother's had enough?'

Karen joined in. 'You're getting on my nerves. What's wrong with you?'

'Well . . .'

'Well what? Out with it.'

Damon glanced at Sheila. 'I've been thinking about whether to tell you this or not. But I will. The police have got Pat in for questioning. About an . . . attack . . . on a woman last night.'

'The attack on mum?' asked Karen.

'I dunno, do I? But it could be if they know the addresses.'

Sheila showed the first signs of animation she'd shown all day. 'No, it wasn't Pat.'

'You said you had no idea who,' said Bobby.

'I might not know who it was, but I know who it wasn't. And it wasn't Pat.'

'Who was it then?' asked Karen.

'If only we knew.'

'If only it had never happened.'

Bryant went to interview Sandra. He came straight to the point.

'What's the set-up here?' he asked.

'It's straightforward. Three of us share a house.'

'And you share a room with Pat Hancock?'

'Not any more.'

'Fallen out, have you?'

'It happens to couples. Even if they're married.'

'Why did you move out of his room?'

'What's this about?'

'Hancock had scratches on his face. Did you do them?'

'I don't know. I might have done.'

'You might have attacked him, but you don't remember?'

'I might have scratched him when I was defending myself.'

Bryant leaned forward. 'He was attacking you, was he? Is he often violent?'

'It wasn't like that.'

'What was it like then? A playful romp that got out of hand?'

When Bryant had gone, Terry brought Sandra a drink. 'D'you think this is about Sheila?' he asked her.

'Must be.'

'They're barking up the wrong tree, then,' said Terry. 'There's nothing in it as far as Pat's concerned.'

'Isn't there?'

Terry couldn't believe his ears. 'Just because you've fallen out with him, don't go slagging him off to everybody. D'you want him sent down?'

'If he did it, I do.'

'I can't believe you could possibly think it was him.'

'Couldn't it? I had to fight him off last night, didn't I? Just before it happened.'

'That was in anger. I'm sure he's sorry now.'

'Wouldn't this be in anger, this attack? Or don't you see it like that? You're as bad as him when it comes down to it. But then you sit next to him every day in the van, don't you, eyeing the girls. No wonder you stick together.'

'I can't believe this. Not Pat.'

'He was drunk wasn't he? And violent. He could have done it. And whether he did or not I'll never trust him again.'

Being interviewed by the police really made Harry Cross' day. For one thing he could answer all their questions: what Harry didn't know about the activities of his neighbours wasn't worth knowing. For another, he'd have a ready answer the next time anybody dared to call him nosy. Keeping an eye on what was going on wasn't nosiness, it was a public duty. What's more it might help to catch a dangerous criminal.

It was Bryant who came to do the interviewing. 'Did you notice anything out of the ordinary here last night?'

'We're a very close-knit community, here,' said Harry. 'Except the Corkhills, of course. They're not quite the same as us.'

'How's that?'

'They have a bit of a council-house mentality about them I suppose. Whereas the Collins are just the opposite. They think they're a cut above, if you see what I mean.'

'They'd really like to be living over the water,' explained Ralph.

'So would Heather if you ask me,' said Harry. 'We'll not keep her long when she comes back.'

'Back?'

'She's just married. On honeymoon . . .'

Bryant tried to get to the point. 'What about the Grants?'

'Nice family,' offered Ralph.

'Not as good as they think they are,' said Harry, 'She has boyfriends staying over.'

'Mrs Grant?'

'Young Karen. But I suppose she's no different to the rest of the youth of today.'

'And the three next door?'

'They're my lodgers,' said Harry. 'Did you know I've got two houses?'

'What kind of people are they?'

'Quiet enough. Normally.'

Bryant pricked up his ears. 'But not always?'

'Definitely not always,' said Ralph. 'They had such a row in there on Thursday night you could hear them all over.'

'Who was involved in this row?'

'Pat and his girlfriend. He drove out of here like a maniac,' said Harry. 'Looked like he could have killed someone if you ask me.'

'What time was that?'

'Eightish I'd say. What's this about?'

'Just making enquires.'

Bryant went back to Sheila with all this information. She had to steel herself for another interrogation. Karen tried to protect her mother.

'Can't you leave her alone?'

'D'you want to help us find this bloke or not?'

'Shouldn't you have a woman policeman with you?'

'We're supposed to try to but there's a lot on at the moment. And I have heard this kind of thing before. Let's just say I understand.'

Karen looked at him. 'You couldn't possibly understand. You're not a woman, are you?'

'No, but like I said, we've had it before . . .'

'It's not the same, hearing it. You have to be a woman to know what it feels to be looked over when you walk along the street. You have to be a woman to know what it's like to be afraid to walk home alone at night in your own city.'

'It's a question of being careful.'

'Who should be careful? Us or men? Is it fair that *we've* got to be careful just to have ordinary human rights? Careful what we wear, careful where we go. Careful just because we're women. Because if we're not, people like you say we're asking for trouble. We even say it ourselves.'

'Leave it, Karen,' said Sheila.

But there was no stopping Karen. 'You're blaming yourself, aren't you, mum?'

'I just wish I hadn't gone out, that's all.'

'You shouldn't say that. What did you do wrong?'

'Like you said, a woman on her own, asking for trouble.'

'It's not your fault. It's not up to you to stop in, it's up to them . . . men. They've got to stop doing this kind of thing. Don't blame yourself. Him that did this to you is to blame, not you. He's a criminal, mum, and the sooner they find him the better.'

'Yes.' Sheila was beginning to feel a bit better. What Karen said was right. The man had to be caught and as soon as possible. She took a deep breath. 'All right. Let's get this over with.'

'Fact is we've got a neighbour of yours in custody.'

'Patrick Hancock?'

'Bryant was surprised. 'Yes.'

'It wasn't him.'

'Now then, Mrs Grant, how can you know that? You said you didn't see the person who assaulted you.'

'I didn't see him, but I know it wasn't Pat.'

'How do you know that?'

Sheila glanced at Karen. She dropped her head, staring only at her clasped hands.

'D'you want me to go, mum?'

'No . . . no. I need you here. If you don't mind . . .'

Karen looked at Sheila sitting there, hunched and shamefaced, and wanted more than anything to help her. So many times over the years Sheila had been strong for her; now it felt as if their roles were reversed.

'Go 'ead mum,' she said, 'of course I'll stay.'

'Well,' Sheila said, 'I didn't see him. But I felt him. Felt how big he was.' She hesitated. 'Pat's young and hard, I've seen him with his shirt off in the Close. He's got muscles but he's not fat. The man that did it wasn't like Pat. He was podgy.'

Bryant looked at Karen, then at Sheila. 'How d'you know Pat well enough to know this?'

'Like I said, I've seen him.'

Bryant leaned forward, lowering his voice, but they could still hear him clearly. 'You don't by any chance know him better than you say? You haven't had an affair with him?'

'I haven't had an affair with anybody.'

'Nobody?'

'No.'

'We've been making enquiries, Mrs Grant. We've found the taxi driver who picked you up that night. He heard things . . . accusations. There was more going on than you've told us, wasn't there?'

'Yes.'

'Why didn't you tell us? Why wait for us to find out?'

Sheila sighed. 'You don't know what people think, do you? A woman out without her husband. In a pub . . .'

Bryant was opening his notebook. 'I think we'd better get a few details,' he said.

When he'd gone Karen sat holding Sheila's hand. 'Thanks, love,' said Sheila.

'I couldn't leave you on your own.'

'Not just that, what you said about it wasn't my fault. I've been feeling so guilty. It wasn't my fault, was it?'

'We're brought up to think that. Always told to be careful so men don't hurt us. As if we're responsible for what men do.'

'Did I say that to you?'

'Not straight out. But in a way, yes. All that about being careful not to lead boys on.'

'You seem to have learned different.'

'That's university, mum. I'm not just learning about my subject, you know.'

'No. You've grown up this year, haven't you?'

'I thought you'd never notice.'

The sight of police on the Close didn't do anything for Doreen Corkill's peace of mind. Billy, who could recognize a policeman, plain clothes or not, at a distance of a hundred yards, knew what Bryant and Spencer were the minute they got out of their car.

'Come here,' he said to Doreen. 'D'you see what I see over there? That's the police.'

'How d'you know?'

'You can tell from the way they walk. They try and look normal when they're in plain clothes but you can tell. What d'you think they want at the Grants'?'

'How should I know?' said Doreen. 'Unless it's something to do with Damon. He's got time on his hands and you know what they say about idle hands.'

'I just hope they've not come asking about our garage. Have you told anybody how Jimmy got the bricks?'

Doreen was alarmed. 'I haven't. But what if somebody

else has? I wouldn't put it past Harry Cross to go poking his nose in.'

'How would he know the stuff was knock-off?' asked Billy.

'He could have guessed. With it coming in an ordinary van and the way your Jimmy just dropped it and ran.'

Billy peered towards his garage. 'It looks normal enough now it's built.'

'Supposing they ask where the stuff's from? We've no receipts or anything.'

'Say you've just thrown 'em away. Try and carry on as normal, that's best.'

Doreen tried to take Billy's advice and act as normal as possible but it didn't stop her worrying. She didn't want any hint of suspicion falling on any of her family. They'd moved to Brookside Close to get away from that kind of thing. Billy's brother Jimmy was nice enough in himself but he had a criminal record, and the way he made a living was best not talked about. Free garage or no free garage, as far as Doreen was concerned she wouldn't mind if Jimmy never came near again if he was going to get them involved with the law.

Doreen had always tried very hard to be respectable, and never more than now with Rod going ahead with his plans to join the police and Billy all set to start his new job. Now that they'd got the house really nice and Tracy seemed to be getting over that business with Peter Montague things were going very well as far as Doreen was concerned, and she was determined to keep it like that.

Chapter Nine

In the end, it was a perfect stranger who got Pat off the hook. A woman in Childwall spotted the van parked on her grass verge and reported it to the police. Luckily she remembered seeing Pat dump it.

'What did you leave it there for?' Terry asked Pat.

'I knew I was too drunk to drive any more, so I just got out and walked. After all we need the van for our livelihood, don't we?'

'You've lost us a job as it is. I had to get the Clearys to shift a load for Henty.'

'Sorry. I had other things on my mind.'

'I can see you had,' said Terry. Pat looked terrible: unshaven, crumpled and with bloodshot eyes.

'I thought they'd never let me out. Good job this woman saw me dump the van.'

'Lucky for you.'

'Yes.' Pat hesitated. Sheila hadn't been lucky. 'How's Sheila?'

'I haven't seen her myself. Thought it best not. But Damon says she's coping.'

'I hope so. Poor Sheila.'

As soon as he walked into their . . . his . . . bedroom, Pat knew Sandra had moved out for good. She'd shifted her clothes, pictures, make-up, jewellery . . . everything. What there wasn't room for in Kate's bedroom was in suitcases under Terry's bed. She was sleeping in Kate's room even though Damon was still in the middle of the decorating. She plainly preferred bare walls and the smell of paint to sharing a bed with Pat.

The next morning Pat woke from a heavy sleep

reaching for her and found only cold sheets. He was consumed with remorse for what had happened: what a fool he'd been to make all that fuss about Hurrell. He remembered how Sandra had turned to him after the siege, looking to him for comfort and support. That's what he'd give her again, comfort and support. When she'd realized that he'd learned his lesson she'd come back, and he'd never make the same mistake again.

He started by getting up early to make her breakfast before she went to work. But in fact it was Terry, attracted by the unusual smell of grilling bacon, who arrived in the kitchen first.

'What's this in aid of?'

'I guess I'm just kind-hearted.'

'Oh yeah?'

'And I thought if I was nice to Sandra . . .'

'It's no use, Pat. It's over.'

Pat banged some bread in the toaster. 'Don't say that, Terry. I love her.'

'You've got to believe me, you're wasting your time.'

But when Sandra came down she seemed to be pleased. 'Cooked breakfast! Lovely. Whose idea was this?'

'Mine,' said Pat.

'That's lovely.'

'I thought it would help us get back to normal.'

'Normal?' Sandra was cool. 'Is this normal?'

'It could be.'

'Did you make breakfast when we were sharing a room?'

Pat was hurt. 'Nobody's forcing you to eat it.'

'Then I won't.'

'Hey, you can't go without it. You'll be hungry.'

'I'll get something at the hospital.'

Pat tried to be casual. He waved the fresh toast. 'Not as good as this.'

'Isn't it?'

When Sandra had gone, Terry shrugged. 'I did try and warn you.'

'Why is she so touchy?'

'Perhaps it's not just the food she's gone to the hospital for.'

'What d'you mean?'

'You know what I mean.'

Pat was horribly afraid he did. 'Hurrell?'

'Maybe.'

'So I'm not making it up then?'

'I'm saying nothing. Hey, what you doing with that?' Terry pointed at Sandra's plate that Pat had picked up.

'Chucking it.'

'No point in letting good food go to waste. I'll eat it.'

'You're welcome.' Pat looked at his own plate. His stomach churned, the familiar feeling: jealousy. 'Have this as well,' he said, and piled his breakfast on top of Sandra's.

There was one household in the Close where life was going on as normal. Or as normal as it can be when you're newly married. Heather and Nick had spent their honeymoon in Ireland. Heather had introduced Nick to her family and friends, he had introduced her to the joys of sailing. They'd enjoyed all of that; and even more, they'd enjoyed their time alone. It was an altogether satisfactory way to start their new life together.

They'd eaten a lot, drunk a lot and, it seemed, spent a lot. When the taxi from the airport drew up in the Close Nick looked through his pockets but nowhere could he find any money to pay the fare.

'Leave it to me,' said Heather. 'I'll give him a cheque.'

'Funny giving a cheque for such a small amount.'

'What else?'

'All right then.'

When they'd unpacked and had something to eat and loaded the washer, Heather turned her thoughts to the future.

'Work tomorrow. Funny going back as a married woman.'

'Funny or nice?'

Oh, nice. Being married *and* going back to work.'

'Look out, here comes the new audit manager!'

'Yes.' Heather was delighted at the thought.

'I wish I was as pleased at the prospect of my work,' said Nick.

'You don't have to do it. You know what we were talking about on the way home . . . full-time cartoonist. Why not give it a try?'

'It's too hard to break into. I'd be lucky to sell anything in the first year.'

'With my rise we could manage on one salary.'

'It's not as easy as that. I have to pay maintenance for the kids, remember.'

Heather wasn't put off so easily. 'Let's cost it out. I'll do a feasibility study. Where are your bank statements and pay slips?'

'No idea.'

Heather finally ran them to earth in a carrier bag in the back of the wardrobe. She went through them whilst Nick cleared the supper. Even with her trained eye they didn't make much sense.'

'Do you never fill in your chequebook stubs?'

'You know me. Forgetful.'

'Not that you write that many cheques. This is all cash card withdrawals. Every day, more or less, all over Liverpool. Where does it all go?'

'I like to see the kids are OK . . . pocket money and so on.'

'Hundreds of pounds a month?'

'It just goes. You've always known I wasn't good with money.'

Heather laughed. 'You could say that's how we met.' She remembered the evening in the winter when Nick had come round after she had bumped his car. She hadn't believed it was an unpaid phone bill that gave him the excuse to call, but maybe it was. And she'd had to pay for their dinner the first time he took her out. She hadn't minded then, and she didn't really mind now. Except that it gave Nick no option but to keep on with a job he didn't enjoy.

'I don't want to interfere, but if you economized a bit you could afford to stop work. Wouldn't you like to get out of the rat race?'

'Not till the kids are older.'

'At least give up your old flat. It costs you a hundred pounds a month. You don't need it now you're living here.'

'I need somewhere for my furniture. And the kids like it.'

That didn't seem enough reason to Heather but she'd learned to keep quiet where Nick's children were concerned. She's already discovered that being a stepmother was tricky and she didn't want to make another mistake right at the start.

'It's up to you,' she said.

Heather was introduced to the realities of motherhood rather sooner than she had expected. The day after she and Nick came back from honeymoon, Scott Black came to stay. He simply appeared on the doorstep uninvited and unexpected, and came straight out with his request as soon as he saw Nick. 'Can I stay?'

Nick was concerned. 'Is anything the matter, Scott?'

'It's Ginny.'

'Oh dear.' For himself, Nick quite liked Ginny, despite the fact that she could be said to have usurped his place in his ex-wife's affections. He had never blamed Ginny for the break-up of his marriage: the relationship between him and Barbara had broken down long before she came on the scene, and the fact was that she was able to make Barbara happier than he had ever done. But Ginny had never had children of her own, and she was sometimes inclined to come on a bit heavy as a step-parent, especially with Scott. Now Scott had hopes of taking advantage of his father's new comfortable home and new hospitable wife.

'What's Ginny done all of a sudden?' asked Nick.

'She's bossy. I don't mind mum telling me what to do, but she's no right.'

'How exactly has she been bossing you?'

'Washing up. And tidying my room.'

'I thought you and Ruth and Adam had a rota for washing up.'

'It's not just that.'

Heather was sympathetic. 'I think you've missed seeing your dad, haven't you? With us being away and him coming to live up here?'

Scott looked at her hopefully. He'd never been as off her as Ruth had, and now she seemed to understand him very well.

'Yes,' he said.

'Why don't you stay here then,' said Heather. 'I don't mind at all.'

'Go in the kitchen a minute, Scott,' said Nick. 'I think Heather and I need to have a little talk.'

'Let him stay,' said Heather when Scott was out of earshot. 'I get on fine with Adam, Ruth's beginning to thaw, but I hardly know Scott.'

'Don't be taken in. Scott always gets his own way.'

'I want him to stay. We need to get to know each other.'

That evening, Heather came back from work with some good news. She came back to a changed house. For over two years now, ever since she'd thrown Roger out, she'd been used to coming home to peace and quiet. Not any more. When she opened the front door she was met by a blast of heavy metal music from her stereo. Scott had moved some of his records in during the day. It seemed as if he might be intending to stay for some time.

At first, Heather couldn't make herself heard either to Scott or to Nick, who was chopping vegetables in the kitchen. She had to turn the music down before Nick noticed she was there.

'Hello. I'm back.'

He kissed her. 'Hello. Had a good day?'

'Very good. Exceptional.'

'Oh?'

'I have to go to Hong Kong.'

'The perks of being an audit manager!'

'Only . . . what about us?'

'What about us?'

'Here we are, newly married, and in three weeks I'm flying to the other side of the world. Not a good start, is it?'

'Isn't this the kind of thing you've always wanted?' asked Nick.

'Yes.'

'Well then, you can't turn it down. I'll miss you, but we'll have to get used to that, won't we?'

'Thanks.' Heather was showing her appreciation with a kiss, when Scott walked into the kitchen.

'When's supper?'

There were times when having an instant family seemed a bit too instant.

Although they'd eliminated Pat as a suspect, the police were still busy. As well as the taxi driver they interviewed Alun Jones, Matty and Ken Dinsdale. Although they didn't spell out what they were making enquiries about it didn't take Sally Dinsdale long to put two and two together, and when she did she came up to Brookside Close to see Sheila. Sheila thought at first she'd come with sympathy, but it wasn't as simple as all that.

'They've interviewed Ken,' Sally said.

'Why?'

'Somebody told them he'd threatened you. Might've been your lad.'

'And?'

'He didn't do it. It's not him.'

Sheila felt coldly angry. Sally was defending Ken again: would she never learn?

'With you, was he, Wednesday night?'

'No, I was in the hostel.'

'Then how do you know it wasn't him?'

'I just know he wouldn't do it.'

'Why are you so loyal towards him? He beats you up, he threatened me. What makes you so sure he didn't do this?'

'He only hits me because he loves me.'

'Tell me one thing,' said Sheila.

'What?'

'Has he ever raped you?'

'No.'

'I don't believe you.'

'I know he didn't do it to you.'

'But he has to you, hasn't he?'

Sally nodded.

'So what sort of a favour are you doing for other women by covering up for him? If it was him, I want him caught and locked away for a long time.'

Matty didn't dare come up to the house, but he phoned Bobby and asked if they could meet. Luckily Sheila was dozing at the time so there was no awkward questions to answer. 'All right,' said Bobby. 'In the Swan, half seven.'

Bobby had his own reasons for wanting to meet Matty. He wanted to hear from his own friend, someone he trusted, what had really been going on in the pub that night.

'Tell me what happened that night, Matty. I want to know every detail.'

'It'll hurt.'

'Don't I know it? I want to get somebody for this and I don't know where to start. It's a good job our Barry doesn't know about this or there'd be blood all over Liverpool.'

'You've not told him?'

'No, best not. Anyway, Sheila wouldn't want it.'

'No.'

'So tell me what happened in the pub.'

'I'm ashamed, Bob. I was a right bastard that night.'

'Go on.'

'Only when I walked in, it did look as if there was something going on with Sheila and that tutor.'

Bobby shifted sharply. 'You reckon?'

'It looked like it. But now I think it was all him. He definitely fancied Sheila, but she didn't want to know.'

'You sure?'

'She ran away from him, Bobby. And from me.'

'You?'

'Yes. I made a right show of myself. In a way what happened is my fault.'

'How d'you make that out?'

'It was my fault she got out of the cab, wasn't it! It's my fault she was on that road. If she hadn't been he could never have caught her.'

'He? Are you saying you have an idea who it is?'

'You're pushing me Bob. I could be way out.'

'Try it.'

'The guy on the spot with a motive could be Alun Jones.'

Sheila was in bed when Bobby got home.

'I need to talk to you,' he said.

'I've had enough.'

'I need to know things. There were things Matty said . . .'

'Oh.'

'He reckoned Jones fancied you.'

'If he did, what's that to do with all this? Rape isn't about fancying someone, it's about hate.'

'How do you know?'

'I've been talking to Karen. They learn about it, students. So as to protect themselves.'

'I just want to know. Because if it's true he'll wish he'd never been born.'

'Are these threats for my sake or yours?'

'What d'you mean?'

'You make me feel like I'm some property that you've got to defend. I don't want any more violence.'

'I'm trying to do what's best. Best for you.'

'Then leave it to the police. Stop asking, stop accusing. Just leave me alone.'

After that Sheila had another sleepless night. But her mood was changing. She still wanted to hide away, go nowhere, speak to nobody. But now, as well as the shame there was the beginning of anger. It was something to do with something Karen had said. 'Why can't women walk the streets in their own city?' And with Sally's defence of Ken. Sally was too humble, a perpetual victim, but Sheila resolved she wouldn't be. She'd get up, clean everywhere, wash her clothes, care for Claire. Try and make a fresh start.

Rod Corkhill was pleased with the new neighbours. One of them, at least. He'd noticed Ruth the first time she'd ever come up the Close on that disastrous visit on the day of Adam's accident. Now that she came more frequently on visits to her dad he began to look out for her and get to know her better.

Doreen was delighted. Ruth was just the kind of girl-friend she wanted for Rod, not like those scallys who'd come to his party. She was well mannered and well spoken, and if she did dress a bit oddly, Doreen forgave that when she found out that Ruth's mother was an artist.

The person who objected to the friendship was Nick. Neither Ruth nor Heather could understand it: it seemed very out of character for someone who was normally easy-going. Not that his objections made any difference to Ruth's behaviour. She was definitely a young woman with a mind of her own.

She was as interested in Rod as he was in her. Some-times she'd come to the Close straight from school, when she knew her father would still be at work, so as to see him. Tracy wasn't blind to what was going on.

'You fancy her, don't you?'

'What's it to you?'

'She'll make mincemeat of you.'

'Look whose talking. You didn't do too well with that teacher of yours, did you?'

Tracy was hurt. 'Tha's not fair.'

'Mind your own business then.'

True to Julian Tyler's promise, Billy Corkhill got a new car and a bleeper at the start of his new job. To the family the bleeper was like a new toy.

'Just like doctors have,' said Doreen.

'That's right girl, I've joined the professionals.'

'What does it do?' asked Tracy.

'When your dad's wanted for an emergency it makes a noise and a number lights up. Then he has to go and phone in and see what they want.'

'Does it work?'

'Try it,' said Doreen. 'Here you are, here's a ten. Run round the phone box and try.'

Billy's new job was a great relief to Doreen: scrimping and saving had never been in her line. Three days after Billy started she came back from town with presents for them all. A key ring that bleeped when you whistled for it for Billy, a police whistle for Rod, and clothes for Tracy. Billy wasn't very thrilled with the key ring. Even after three days he was beginning to be sick of the sound of bleepers. His seemed to go off every half hour so he was forever running to the phone. He wasn't very thrilled with Rod's whistle either. Billy still hadn't come round to the idea of Rod joining the police and wished that Doreen wouldn't keep bringing it up.

Tracy was appalled at her present. She held the dress Doreen had bought up in front of her. 'I look a right divvie in this,' she said.

'You look lovely,' said Doreen.

'A chip off the old block,' said Billy.

'She looks like a divvie,' said Rod.

In the end, Doreen bowed to the inevitable and gave Tracy the receipt so she could change the dress. 'I hope you're not going to come back with anything too extreme,' she said.

Her hopes were dashed. The next day, Tracy came back from the shops with a parcel, disappeared upstairs for half an hour, and reappeared dressed up and made up to the hilt. It was too much for Billy.

'I don't believe this; what's that you're wearing?' he said.

'Tina looks like this,' said Tracy.

'Tina might, but you're not,' said Doreen. 'Just go upstairs and put on something sensible.'

'What d'you want me to do, wear me school uniform for ever?' asked Tracy.

'It'd be better than that.'

'All right,' said Tracy.

Doreen couldn't believe it would be that easy, and it wasn't. When Tracy came down again, she was in her school uniform right enough, but with the skirt hitched up, and the blouse undone in a way that made her look as if she was auditioning for a job in a night-club. Doreen took one look and gave in. 'All right,' she said. 'You win.'

'You mean I can wear me other clothes?' asked Tracy.

'If you must. Just go easy on the eye make-up, that's all.'

'Oh mum,' said Tracy, 'I love you.' She flung her arms round Doreen, and gave her a hug. 'Thanks mum.'

Watching Tracy run upstairs, Doreen didn't know whether to laugh or cry. Sometimes Tracy was fifteen going on five, and that was all right. It was when she was fifteen trying to be twenty that Doreen worried. Tracy was a pretty girl, the sort men would take advantage of if they could. Doreen only hoped that Tracy had learnt her lesson from that Peter Montague business and would stick to lads of her own age in the future.

Despite his father's objections, Rod had gone ahead and

sent up for the application forms for the police. He was leaving school at the end of term and looking forward to earning a bit of money. He'd only stayed on in the sixth form to please his mother. At one time, Doreen had had hopes of Rod maybe doing some A levels, and going on to college. Rod knew there'd never been any chance of that, and now that it had taken him three goes to get his five O levels even Doreen had to lower her sights. As far as she was concerned, the police seemed a good second best, particularly when she found out what money he'd be getting. She was behind him all the way.

The same wasn't true of Billy. He peered over Rod's shoulder as he started on the form.

'Better not mention me and your mum are married, or they might turn you down.'

'Billy!' said Doreen.

'When do they give you the test about taking bribes?'

'You can laugh when we're both due to retire at the same time,' said Rod.

'How d'you make that out?'

'Twenty odd years and I'll be retiring with a full pension.'

'It'll not be much fun when it's tippling down and you're patrolling the dock road in the middle of the night.'

'If I get in,' said Rod.

Doreen was indignant. 'What d'you mean, if you get in? You're tall enough.'

'They go into your background. What about Uncle Jimmy? And dad being charged with assaulting the teacher?'

'None of that's to do with you,' said Billy. 'If they turn you down because of that, I'm writing to somebody.'

'Like who?' asked Doreen.

Billy was nonplussed, but only for a moment. 'Our MP. If I knew who he was.'

By now, the news that Annabelle was hoping to become a

magistrate was all round the Close. Rod took his form across to her house.

'I'm applying to join the police,' he explained.

'Jolly good,' said Paul.

'I'm sure it's a very good career,' said Annabelle, 'and well paid nowadays.'

'They've not taken me yet. I need somebody to put on my form.'

'Give you a reference?'

'With you being a JP and that,' said Rod.

'I'm not quite there yet,' said Annabelle, 'but I'd be delighted to testify as to your character.'

'Great,' said Rod. 'I'll put your name on the form then, shall I?'

'Yes. And good luck.'

'Thanks. Er . . . same to you.'

Damon was getting on well with the decorating for Pat, Sandra and Terry. He enjoyed doing a good job, seeing shabby walls and paintwork come up fresh and bright, and he was glad to have somewhere to go that kept him out of his mother's way. Over the last few days, Sheila had emerged from her mood of withdrawn passivity to being hyperactive, as if by keeping busy she could make the time go faster and keep her thoughts at bay. At the moment it was impossible to sit down in the Grants' without being moved to make way for the vacuum cleaner or given a duster and a tin of polish and told to lend a hand.

The only snag as far as Damon was concerned was that the decorating wasn't going to last for ever. So he was particularly pleased when Terry said he might be able to find him a job for the summer.

'What kind of a job?'

'Selling ice cream out of a van. Some of Vicki's relatives are looking for somebody. It could put a few bob in your pocket.'

'I'd feel a right divvie.'

'Can afford not to, can you?'

'No, I can't afford not to. I'll do it. When do I start?'

But Terry came back from Vicki's with bad news. 'Sorry Damon, they don't want you.'

'They don't know me.'

'It's not you personally. It's anybody like you.'

'What's that mean?'

'They want a girl. They reckon girls sell more ice creams than lads, don't ask me why.'

'I could sell ice cream to the Eskimos.'

'I know that, Damon, you know that, but they don't. Far as they're concerned they want a girl and that's it. Unless you're thinking of having the operation you've no chance.'

Damon was bitter. 'That's it, isn't it, no chance. Not even for a piddling little job like that. I don't know why I bother trying.'

'Something'll turn up.'

'If you believe that you'll believe anything.'

Sheila had just finished doing the house through for the second time in two days and gone upstairs for a sleep, when Teresa called. Bobby answered the door, shocked, as Sheila had been, by the change in Teresa.

'Is Sheila in?' she asked.

'She's having a lie-down.'

'Oh.'

'She needs it. She's not had much sleep since . . .'

'No.'

'So I'd sooner not wake her.'

'It's all right.'

'Still, I'm here, aren't I?'

'Yes.' Teresa took a deep breath. 'I suppose you'll do.'

'Well, if it's to talk about . . . you know . . . it's better she's not here really. We try not to keep on bringing it up.'

'Yes, I can understand that. I wouldn't have come, but I didn't know where else I could go.'

'What is it, Teresa! Is it Matty?'

'Yes. You won't believe this, Bobby, it seems incredible, but I've had the police round.'

'I suppose they have to make their enquiries.'

'They want to know where Matty is. As if I'd know. And they were funny. As if they think it was him.'

'Never.'

'They've been talking to people at the pub. It seems he was off his head with drink. They say he threatened Sheila.'

'He was upset.'

'And that he followed her out.'

'They're wasting their bloody time. Why don't they ask the taxi driver where he dropped Matty off? That'll give Matty an alibi.'

'Oh Bobby, I'm frightened.'

'What for? You know Matty. He'd never do a thing like that.'

'He's changed, Bobby. I did know Matty until a few weeks ago. But now he's not the same at all.'

Chapter Ten

It was now over a week since Sandra had sent her report on Cribbs-Baker's work to the newspaper and she'd heard nothing. She tried asking Karen, in her role as a student of media studies, if she should do anything more.

'Leave it a bit,' said Karen. 'They're probably following it up. Or waiting to see if it fits in with anything else they're considering.'

Sandra had taken to spending as much time as possible at work. There she was kept busy, too busy to worry about what was happening to her report, and besides, she got the occasional glimpse of Tony Hurrell, and although their relationship was now confined to formal exchanges, that was better than nothing. It was only now that she wasn't seeing so much of Tony that Sandra realized how much she missed him. Perhaps Pat had been right all along and there had been more than just the campaign between them.

At home things were very sticky indeed. Pat was behaving like a whipped puppy. He hung about trying to catch Sandra, asking how she was, constantly offering to wash up or make her something to eat or carry her bag. She avoided him as much as she could, not coming out of her room until he'd gone downstairs, and eating at the hospital to avoid the strained mealtimes. Days off were the worst. When all three of them were in together, the house suddenly seemed very small, and it was only Terry's tact and good humour that stopped things blowing up into another row.

Terry was piggy in the middle, sympathetic to both parties. He thought he had a good idea of what was going on for Sandra and one day he broached it.

'You missing this Tony fella?'

'Yes. But he let me down.'

'Doesn't stop you missing him, though?'

'No.'

These days Terry wasn't finding Pat very good company in the van. Either they drove along in gloomy silence, or Pat discussed endless strategies for winning Sandra back. Terry gave what advice he could. 'Leave her alone, Pat. It's all you can do. It's the hardest thing in the world, but you've got to let go.'

The best escape from the tension in the house was the garden, and Sandra suddenly became an obsessional weeder. Even Harry was impressed by the improvement she'd made with a couple of days of hard work.

She was in the back garden digging away with her trowel when Tony Hurrell came round to see her. 'You seem busy,' he said.

Sandra looked up, smiling with surprise and pleasure. 'Hi . . .' she said. Then she remembered that they weren't on the same side any more. 'What brings you here?' she asked.

'Well, not to beat about the bush, I've had the press on to me. Asking about Cribbs-Baker.'

'Ah . . . I sent them some material.'

Tony wasn't pleased. 'Why? You knew I'd be against it. I said so.'

'I thought I might do it without you having to be involved.'

'You thought what? I'm in it up to the neck. Why else would they have rung me up. And they've been talking to Cribbs-Baker.'

'I had to do something. I didn't want just to give up.'

'*You* didn't want to. What about what'll happen to my job?'

'Don't blame it all on me. You began all this. If it wasn't for you I'd never have become involved.'

'I've changed my mind, haven't I.'

Sandra was furious. 'Just like that, eh? And has he

139

stopped his operations? Is all this because he leaned on you in the car park?'

'He talked sense . . .'

Sandra knew then. 'Has a job come up?' she asked.

Tony had the grace to look shamefaced. 'Yes.'

'I dare say Cribbs-Baker's going to write you a good reference?'

'Since you ask, yes. But not if this story gets printed.'

'So he's bought you off.'

'It's not as simple as that. He's one of a host of men, most of whom think the same as him. They're powerful and conservative, and I've got to get in with them if I want to work. And I do want to work. I think I have something to offer. You know what a lot of surgeons are like, walking along as if they owned the place.'

'Cribbs-Baker to name but one.'

'Right. And you know I'm not like that. I try and treat patients as whole people, not just as a part of the body.'

Sandra was silent. She knew she'd lost. Tony looked at her. 'I don't want this. You're the last person in the world I want to argue with. Why d'you think I came round? Don't write me off.'

Sandra heard the plea in his voice. So there was something personal in this for him too. But knowing that, hoping that, didn't stop her being angry. 'You're writing this campaign off,' she said.

'We've taken it as far as we can.'

'What are you asking me to do?'

'If the newspaper gets in touch with you then say your position's changed. That's what I did . . .'

Sandra gave up. 'You'll be moving away?' She felt unbearably sad at the thought.

'That's right. At least it'll give you and Pat a chance.'

It's too late for that, thought Sandra, but she didn't say so. There seemed no point. Tony was going and that was that. It seemed as if they'd wasted all that time together with the case records and now it was too late to get to know one another. 'Well, good luck,' she said.

'I'll miss you,' said Tony.

'Yes.'

'If the newspaper rings you up . . .'

'I won't withdraw,' said Sandra. 'Something good's got to come out of all this.'

On his way down the Close, Tony passed Alun Jones coming to see Sheila. Luckily for Alun Karen opened the door or he wouldn't even have got inside the house. Karen left him in the hallway whilst she called her mother and Sheila came downstairs to find him standing awkwardly by the door.

'Hello, Sheila,' he said. 'I've come to offer you an apology.'

'Oh yes?'

'For the things I said. I realize now there were no grounds for what I hoped.'

'Bit late, isn't it?'

'I heard what happened.'

Sheila's calm cracked. 'It seems like everybody has.'

'The police questioned me.'

'What did they find out?'

'I'm in the clear. I've got an alibi. I went straight from the pub to a friend's, you see.'

'Lucky you.'

'If only there was something I could do.'

'There isn't.'

'You didn't come to the last session of the class . . .'

'Sorry I didn't send a note.'

'I didn't mean . . . I just wanted to say I hope you'll continue your education. Don't waste what you've got.'

'It's taking me all my time to keep going just at the minute.'

'Yes . . . but perhaps in the future . . .'

'Perhaps.'

Damon had finished the decorating for Sandra. He was back to the old routine of staying in bed late and looking vainly through the job ads, with going to sign on as the highlight of his life. It didn't seem fair: he tried hard enough, he did good work when he got the chance, but no matter how hard he tried, it seemed impossible to get fixed up. And it was going to get harder every year as more and more kids left school and signed on. Damon was by nature easy-going and optimistic, but sometimes he felt very low indeed.

It didn't help that Karen got the job selling ice cream that he'd been refused. Why should she have work when he hadn't, just because she was a girl? She was a student, she'd got a grant, she'd got a future. She didn't really need the work: for her it was just something to fill in the summer with.

Karen's first outing with the van was to Croxteth Hey Day with Vicki. Terry was a bit anxious about the whole thing.

'Be careful,' he said. 'Don't let any fellows give you the eye.'

'I wouldn't worry, Terry,' said Sandra. 'They'll be quite safe inside the van.'

'It's as good as a mobile chastity belt,' said Vicki.

The Corkhills were getting ready to go to the Hey Day too, and Rod was taking a lot of trouble about it. He'd arranged to meet Ruth there, and as this was the first time he'd made a proper arrangement with her as opposed to meeting her by chance on the Close, he was keen to make a good impression.

Nick and Heather's decision to go to the Hey Day was altogether more last minute. Heather had come downstairs after a weekend lie-in to find that the kitchen was littered with the remains of Scott's midnight feast, the sink was full of dirty dishes, and the radio had been left on all night. By now this was no more than she expected. The fact was that Heather was not finding it easy to adjust to life with Scott. She wasn't used to living with anybody else, and particularly not with a teenager who borrowed her things, messed the place up, used all the hot water

just when she was planning to have a bath and mono-
polized the telephone.

During the week, she survived by being out most of
the time in the comparative peace of her office, surrounded by people who, unlike Scott, listened to what
she said and paid attention to her requests. Weekends
were the difficult time, and she feared that a day at home
together would be more than her frayed nerves would
stand. So she was delighted when Nick suggested a family
outing.

'The only thing is,' she said, 'will Scott be keen?'

'I'll offer him a carrot,' said Nick. 'I'll let him take my
camera.'

'Isn't that more like a bribe,' said Heather.

'It's a carrot,' said Nick. 'I know one when I see one.'

What Nick didn't expect was to see Ruth at the Hey
Day with Rod Corkill. He spotted them when he was
buying ice cream from a far-from-expert Karen. 'Stand
back,' said Karen, 'or you'll get ice cream down your
front.' Nick peered over her shoulder and across the van.
'Do I see my daughter over there?' he asked.

'With Rod Corkhill? Yes,' said Karen. 'Everybody's
here, aren't they?'

When Nick returned with the ice creams and told
Heather what he'd seen she was amused. 'After you told
her not to,' she said. 'How could she! gross disobedi-
ence. Just remember the carrot.'

'What?'

'Your liberal father number,' said Heather.

'All right,' said Nick. 'You win.'

As far as Rod was concerned, the day was a great success.
He got to know Ruth a lot better, and the more he got to
know her, the more he liked her. 'My mum likes you
too,' he said.

'Would she if she knew my mum lived with another
woman?'

'What d'you mean, lives with?'

'You know, like a couple. Like husband and wife.'

'In bed, you mean?'

'Well, they share a room.'

'I don't know that she'd quite grasp that. Might be as well. What's it like for you?'

Ruth shrugged. 'I'm just glad my mum's got someone she gets on with.'

'Couldn't she get on with your father?'

'Well, he had some problems. But we're not here to talk about that, are we?'

Tracy took advantage of Scott having his dad's camera to have her new clothes recorded for posterity. Not once or twice, but several times, in different places and in different poses. She decided she quite liked this modelling business, even if her mother would interfere. 'Make sure you get all of her in the picture,' said Doreen.

'He's getting the background right,' said Tracy.

'Her dad leaves the feet off a lot of the time, and those are her new shoes. I want them in the photo.'

The only person who didn't really enjoy the day out was Billy, and that was because he didn't get much chance to. His bleeper went about five minutes after they'd got there. 'Oh no,' said Doreen, 'not on a Sunday afternoon.'

'I'm supposed to be on call all the time,' said Billy. 'Only I didn't realize it'd mean all the time.'

'Well, at least this one's not in the middle of the night,' said Doreen. 'That's the worst.'

'You're telling me,' said Billy. He felt as if he hadn't had a proper night's sleep in weeks.

'Do you have to go?'

'No choice, have I? You know what Mr Tyler said. He only likes good workers. Will you be all right on your own, Doe?'

'Have to be, won't I?'

It was easy for Doreen to be brave in broad daylight when she was surrounded by a lot of people; it wasn't so easy in the dead of night when Billy was out, and every creak of a floorboard might have been an intruder. Hearing about what had happened to Sheila didn't do anything for Doreen's peace of mind. If that kind of thing could happen to a neighbour then it could happen to her. Doreen decided to take steps to defend herself. Later that week she arrived back from the shops with a bag full of locks.

'What's all this?' Rod asked.

'What's it look like?'

'Looks like you're turning us into Fort Knox.'

'Or you are.'

'What d'you mean?'

'I was thinking you might put them on for me. Call it your contribution to law and order, practising for the police.'

'Ah, but I'll get a good wage for that.'

'I'll give you a quid.'

'One fifty.'

'All right.'

Unfortunately Doreen forgot just one thing: to warn Billy. He was out on a job when Rod fitted the locks and he arrived back in the small hours to find he couldn't get into his own house. He rattled the door and then tried one of the windows. 'Doe, what's going on?'

Doreen woke to the sound of the rattling and was terrified. She sat up in bed, wondering if Rod would hear if she banged on the wall. Billy called again. 'You there, Doe? It's me, Billy. What's going on around here?'

Doreen and Rod went down together to let him in. 'What is this?' asked Billy. 'Am I out so much you've forgotten who I am?'

Sheila was beginning, bit by bit, to feel better. She still wouldn't go out very far from home but she was willing to talk to people on the Close and she had begun to sleep better. The police were continuing with their enquiries, but there wasn't much more either Sheila or Bobby could do to help them.

Now that the worst was over Bobby began to find that time hung heavy on his hands. If he tried to do too much to help Sheila, she got irritated with him and reminded him she wasn't an invalid; and yet there wasn't much else for him to do at home. So he wasn't altogether displeased to get a telephone call from Dave Butler, the shop steward at Bragg's, even though the phone call was disturbing. It seemed from what Dave was saying that in Bobby's absence George Williams had taken over the handling of the strike, and he wasn't being very sympathetic to the men.

Bobby decided that compassionate leave or not he'd better get down to the office and find out what was going on. He arrived there to find George sitting behind his desk. In his chair.

'What're you doing here?' George asked when Bobby appeared. 'I didn't expect to see you for another couple of weeks.'

'So I see,' said Bobby.

'Just keeping your seat warm. How's Sheila?'

'Coping. But there's nothing I can do at home, so I thought I'd find out what Dave Butler's on about.'

'No need; I'm handling the dispute at Bragg's. Best thing for you'd be to get off home and look after Sheila for another couple of weeks.'

Bobby was feeling angry but he tried to keep it light. 'Come on, George, get out of me chair.'

'It's not your chair. Not at the minute it's not.'

'How d'you make that out?'

'The National Executive suspended you for four weeks. I know I didn't put it like that, I couldn't bring myself to under the circumstances. So I changed it on my own initiative to compassionate leave. Out of consideration for you.'

'Consideration for me? You got me out the way so you could welsh on the lads at Bragg's whilst I wasn't here.'

'So I could enact the decision of the Executive Committee and get them back to work.'

146

'You used the fact my wife has been raped to get me out of the way.'

'You'd've been out of the way anyway, Bobby. A month's suspension. Remember?'

Matty Nolan had finished with Liverpool. He had no job and no prospect of one; no home except a bed in the Seamen's Mission, and Mo refused to see him. And the police were on his back.

He went to see Teresa. She wasn't in when he called and although he still had his key he didn't like to go into the empty house, so he waited across the road until she came back. He appeared behind her as she fumbled to put the key in the lock.

'I'll do it,' he said.

It was the first time he'd seen Teresa since the day she'd made a show of herself in the Return to Learn class at Sheila's and, like Sheila, he was shocked at the change in her. But if that made him feel sorry for Teresa, he took good care to block it out. As far as Matty was concerned his mind was made up. There was no turning back; he'd gone too far for that.

'This is still your house,' said Teresa.

'I've not come to come back,' said Matty. 'I'm just going to pick up some stuff.'

Teresa looked at the bag he'd put on the floor. 'Are there dirty clothes in there?'

'Just a few. I've done some at the launderette.'

Teresa picked up the bag. 'I'll sort it out.'

'No you don't. You don't get me back that way.'

'It's a good drying day. You could pick it up tomorrow.'

'I won't be here tomorrow. I'll be a long way away. I'm leaving, for good. Leaving all this behind. And that includes you and Sheila Grant.'

'And your own children.'

Matty was upset but he wasn't going to show it or let it stop him. 'I've got to make a fresh start. When I find a job and somewhere to stay I'll try and send some money. But you won't know where I am. I'll just be one more missing person. Just forget about me, pretend I never was. Got it?'

'I can't do that, Matty, not after twenty years.'

'There's people to help you isn't there? Talk to the priest, isn't that what they're for?'

'I can't talk to the priest, I'd be ashamed. I couldn't tell him what I think sometimes.' Teresa was looking down at her hands. 'You know what they say about mortal sin.'

Matty knew what she meant by mortal sin. She was trying to tell him she might give in to the ultimate act of despair. But he didn't believe her, it was emotional blackmail. 'None of that daft talk. I'm going, get that into your head.'

'With your fancy woman, I suppose. She's took you back?'

'No, and she won't. I've lost her. She'll move on.'

For a moment Teresa had hope. 'Matty, if you did come back . . .'

'No. It wouldn't work. You'd try all right, but every time we had a row you'd bring up Mo and what I'd done. I couldn't stand that. I'd end up sticking a knife in you, I really would.'

'That's not you Matty. I know you.'

'Not any more you don't. I've changed. This has changed me, I'm not like I was.' Matty got his keys out of his pocket and put them down on the table. 'I won't be needing these again,' he said. 'I don't live here any more. It was a different bloke lived here.'

The keys were still on the table when the police called that afternoon. Teresa hadn't had the heart to move them, it would have seemed so final. Detective Sergeant Spencer spotted them at once.

'Do you always leave your keys on the table?' she asked.

'No.'

'They are yours?'

'They're Matty's. He's made me a present of them.'

'When?'

'This morning. Dinner-time. He handed them in like this was a hotel. It's only been his home for twenty years.'

Detective Sergeant Spencer was sympathetic. 'He's changed, has he?'

'He has. Wouldn't let me near him, wouldn't let me even touch his washing. Wouldn't think of coming back.'

'Why not?'

'He said he'd be afraid to. Said he'd be afraid of knifing me. It's terrible what that woman's done to him. My Matty would never have talked like that.'

'People change, Mrs Nolan. He's been through a lot.'

'Yes. And it's all her fault, that Mo Francis. Though he blames Sheila.'

'Sheila Grant?'

'Yes. He went mad. Said he'd never forgive her for what she'd done.'

Detective Sergeant Spencer got her notebook out.

'He actually said that?'

'Yes. Is it important?'

'It could be. You see he was one of the last to see Sheila, and he was angry with her then. They left together in a taxi, Sheila gets out of the taxi, your husband takes the taxi on. He said he went to a pub, but that's not what the taxi driver says. He says your husband stopped him just round the corner. Why didn't your husband tell us that? And if he went to the pub, how is it nobody saw?'

Teresa shook her head, disbelieving. 'What are you trying to say?'

'What does it add up to?'

'That Matty did that? To Sheila? I can't believe it. . . .'

'You said he hated her.'

'Yes, but . . .'

'It's hate fuels rape, not lust, as people think. Hate,

149

and fear for women in general or one particular woman. What does that add up to, Mrs Nolan?'

Annabelle was feeling pleased with life. That morning she'd got the letter she'd been waiting for, the one that told her she'd been accepted for consideration as a magistrate. She was eager to tell someone that news and was delighted when Sheila called round.

But Sheila had come with an agenda of her own. She listened to Annabelle politely, offered her congratulations, and then introduced the subject casually.

'Have you heard from Lucy recently?'

'No. Have you heard from Barry?'

'No. We never do. One postcard saying '*Vive la France*', that's all. If it hadn't been for Lucy, we wouldn't even know where he was.'

'Oh.' There was an awkward silence. The fact that Annabelle's daughter Lucy and Sheila's son Barry were living together in France was a source of embarrassment to them both. Mentioning it brought back unhappy memories of how it had come about. Barry had set off in the hopes of selling a load of videos which he didn't have any papers for, and Lucy had gone with him on impulse after the calamitous end of her affair with a married man. Neither Annabelle nor Sheila wanted to dwell on what had happened before Lucy and Barry had gone, or on what they might be getting up to now.

'Well, if you've not heard I've had no need to worry,' said Sheila.

'Worry about what?'

'About Barry hearing about what's happened to me.'

'I'm so sorry about that,' said Annabelle. 'Is there anything I can do?'

'Nothing except not tell Lucy. I just don't want our Barry to know anything about it.'

'I can understand that,' said Annabelle. 'It must be very embarrassing.'

'Yes,' said Sheila. That wasn't really the reason at all

but she was content to let Annabelle think it was. It seemed too difficult to explain the real reason. Barry was her eldest, that baby who'd come along when she was only nineteen, and, if she was honest, he was still her favourite child, despite all the trouble they'd had with him. He loved her too, and would defend her with his fists if need be. What Sheila was really afraid of was Barry's response if he heard about the attack on her. She suspected he might get on the first plane home and come seeking vengeance, and she didn't want that. What good would more violence do?

'So you won't mention it?' she said.

Annabelle smiled. 'You can count on me. And Paul. Not a word will pass our lips, I can assure you of that.'

Chapter Eleven

Despite what he'd told Teresa, Matty didn't leave Liverpool straight away. He couldn't bring himself to go without seeing Bobby. They'd been mates since they'd first started school together and had stuck together through thick and thin. He couldn't leave until he'd said goodbye.

He rang from a call box and arranged to meet Bobby on the recreation ground. He didn't want to go anywhere anybody might see him or recognize him. And he wanted plenty of space, somewhere he could keep on the move so his feelings wouldn't show. None of this was easy.

'What's this about then?' asked Bobby.

'I'm leaving,' Matty said, 'and I'm never coming back.'

'Matty lad, you can't.'

'Why not?'

'You've a wife and three kids.'

'Not any more. I left them, don't you remember?'

'Come on. You couldn't face Teresa because you didn't have a job or any self-respect, that's all.'

'I was in love with Mo.'

'You thought you were because she gave you something to think about when you had nothing else. You're like a lot of others. The unemployed get divorced twice as often as anybody else. You're not the first this has happened to and you won't be the last.'

'If I'm not, how does that help me? It still leaves me with nothing.'

'So how will leaving help? You've nothing anywhere else, have you?'

Matty was silent and Bobby knew he was winning. 'Don't give in, Matty,' he said. 'Fight back. Phone Teresa. She'll have you back, I'm sure she will.'

For a moment Matty found the prospect very appealing, but then his doubts came back. 'It wouldn't work. There's too much water under the bridge. Every time we had a row she'd drag it up and throw it in me face. And then there'd be no knowing what would happen.'

'Teresa wouldn't do that.'

'She'd not feel safe. If I got stuck in a pub with you and was late getting home she'd think I was with another woman . . .'

'When all the time it was another man.'

Matty laughed, and laughing made it seem possible. 'All right, it's worth a try. Have you got any money for the phone?'

The police had come back to go through the details again with Teresa.

'Your husband left home some weeks ago, is that right?'

'Yes.'

'He went to live with another woman?'

'Yes.'

'He was upset when this relationship broke up?'

'Yes.'

'That's when he blamed Mrs Grant?'

'If you say so.'

'It's not just our say-so, a lot of people heard him. He was saying terrible things in the pub.'

'Are you saying you think he might've . . .'

'You've seen him, Mrs Nolan. You told us he'd talked about knifing you.'

'He didn't mean it.'

'How can you be sure of that? People change, you know.'

'He wasn't himself.'

'No, he was angry. And when a man's angry, he might

153

do anything. You might not be safe, Mrs Nolan.'

'I don't believe this.'

'You'd better believe it. People can do strange things when they're angry.'

Teresa was frightened. 'Matty was angry.'

Detective Constable Bryant was paternal. 'Don't worry, we'll get him before he gets anywhere near you. We'll have a man here all the time until we've picked him up.'

When Matty rang from a call box near the recreation ground Teresa picked up the phone at once. She listened, looked at Bryant, found her voice. 'Hello Matty,' she said.

Bryant waited till she put the phone down. Then he switched on his radio. 'Stand by,' he said, 'he's on his way.'

Bobby dropped Matty off at the end of the road. 'Sure you don't want me to come with you?' he said.

'No. I'd be better going on me own. Then it'll be just me and Teresa.'

'Best of luck then,' said Bobby.

'I'll be all right. Why else would she say she'd see me?'

Matty walked up the road. Just as he lifted his hand to knock on his front door the police arrested him.

They took Teresa down to the police station in a separate car. She was glad of that, she didn't want to look Matty in the face. Could it be true, what they said about him? Had he done that to Sheila? Two weeks ago when Matty had left home she'd thought the worst that could happen to her had happened, but this was much worse. Matty was in police custody and she was the one who'd put him there. She'd let him come to the house knowing they were waiting for him. She'd let him be arrested on his own doorstep. . . .

Detective Constable Bryant was giving Matty a hard time.

'I'm talking about Sheila Grant. You hated her, didn't you? She'd spoilt it for you, hadn't she, you and Mo?'

'Yes, but . . .'

'Because of that you got out of the taxi that night to go after her, to get your own back.'

'That's not why. I didn't have the money for the fare.'

'Not fair was it, they had money didn't they, while you were on the dole. Because of her you had nothing, no money, no wife, no Mo . . .?'

'All right, I had nothing. And I blamed Sheila, yes it was her that caused it. But I didn't . . . I didn't . . .'

'Didn't mean to rape her? What did you mean then, just to teach her a lesson? But it got out of hand, didn't it? Didn't it? . . .'

Matty was left alone with his thoughts. He couldn't believe this was really happening to him. Only an hour or two ago he'd been talking to Bobby and there'd seemed a way out of his pit of despair. Now he was in it deeper than ever. Why wouldn't they believe him? How could he convince them?

Detective Sergeant Spencer came next.

'Where's your boss?' he asked her.

'He's not my boss, I'm his. Wrong way round, is it?'

'I didn't think . . .'

'You didn't think what? That women should be giving orders?'

'What's this about?'

'Maybe you don't like women, Matty. Not women with minds of their own.'

'What are you getting at?'

'It's ordinary men rape women, Matty. Not monsters. Ordinary men who're afraid of women. Men like you.'

The more Teresa thought about it, the more she began to regret what she'd done. Where was Matty? What was happening to him? What were they saying to him? It was all a mistake, he shouldn't be here.

She tried to get the police to listen to her.

'I want to make a statement.'

'Why?'

'Matty didn't do it.'

155

'How d'you know? You weren't there were you?'

'I've told lies. He never had an affair with that Mo.'

'A lot of other people say he did.'

'I just wanted to get at him. I made it all up.'

'What we're interested in is facts, not what you feel.'

'You don't believe me, do you? You're not listening. You're not going to let him out, are you?'

'What do you think, Mrs Nolan?'

Teresa went for help to the only people she could think of, the Grants. She was shaking all over by the time she got to Brookside Close. Shelia sat her down whilst Karen made a cup of tea.

'I shouldn't really have come here,' said Teresa.

'Where else?'

'After what they're saying about Matty . . .'

'Matty didn't do it.'

'How d'you know?'

'I just know.' But really Sheila didn't know. The memory of what had happened was fainter now: she could remember the darkness and the smell and the hands . . . but whose hands? She tried to be convincing for Teresa. 'It'll be all right, you'll see.'

Teresa tried to believe Sheila but she couldn't. How could anything be all right after this? What right had she to ask Sheila for help after what Shelia had been through? 'You're right,' she lied. 'I'd best go home in case they bring him.'

Bobby took Teresa home. The house was empty, the children were staying with their grandmother. Bobby hesitated, not wanting to leave Teresa on her own.

'Sure you'll be all right?'

'Sure.'

'If there's anything I can do, anything at all, just give us a ring. I'll be round right away.'

'I'll be all right.'

It was only after she'd closed the door that she allowed herself to cry.

*

The police were trying the soft technique on Matty.

'What made you get out of the taxi?'

'I couldn't pay the fare. I was embarrassed.'

'Embarrassed? You've been on the dole long enough to get used to that.'

'Easy Pete,' said Spencer. 'Maybe he was ashamed about the fare. Maybe he was going to catch Sheila to say he was sorry.'

'I never saw Sheila. I went to the pub.'

'Catholic aren't you? Used to confessing?'

'Gonna offer me a priest?'

'No need for a priest, we'll do. Try and tell us the truth.'

'I have.'

'Guilt's a terrible thing, you can't carry it inside you. Time to let it out, Matty. Time to confess.'

Bobby couldn't stop worrying about Teresa. He shared it with Sheila. 'The house was so empty, she'll miss the kids and Matty. I shouldn't have left her on her own.'

'Give her a ring.'

'D'you think that's enough? You can hide things on the phone. She could be feeling terrible and still not say. I think I'd better go round.'

'All right.'

Bobby knocked and shouted for five minutes before Teresa opened the door. When she did she didn't invite him in.

'All right love?' he asked.

'Have you got some news?'

'No, we've not heard a thing. Are they still keeping Matty?'

'Yes.'

'I don't like you being on your own and that.'

'I'm not on my own.'

'How's that?'

'Our Stephen came back. He didn't stay at his nan's. He's keepin' me going.'

'Well if you're sure.'

'Honest. I'm best left here.'

Teresa closed the door and had the house to herself again. She felt a bit guilty about pretending to Bobby that Stephen was there, but she wanted to be left alone. She couldn't face anybody just now, not even her oldest friends. She was at rock bottom. If Matty hadn't done what they said he had, what kind of a wife was she? She'd betrayed him, given him away, let the police take him. And if he had . . . but that didn't bear thinking about.

Matty's ordeal came to an end halfway through the evening. He was sitting in the interview room, guarded as ever by a silent policeman, waiting, just waiting, for the next bit of his interrogation, when Spencer came in.

'Mr Nolan, there've been some developments.'

Matty knew they must be to his benefit: they'd never called him Mr here before.

'You've got somebody else?'

'Yes.'

'He's owned up?'

'Not quite. But he was committing an offence and we believe it's not the first.'

'Has he confessed?'

'He will do, we'll see to that.'

The first thing Matty did when they finally let him out was go to the telephone. He'd ring Teresa first and then go home. He'd never wanted his home so much in all his life. After all he'd been through he was crystal-clear that home was where he wanted to be and home was where he wanted to stay. He'd ask Teresa to have him back and they'd put all this behind them. He didn't want to go away, that was no way to make a fresh start. He'd make one here.

Teresa let the telephone ring. She didn't dare to answer it. By now all hope was gone. She knew who it would be:

158

the police. If they had anything to tell her, let them come. Bad news travels fast, she'd know it soon enough anyway. She switched on the radio to drown out the noise.

She tried praying but that was no help. She didn't deserve help, a woman who'd done what she had done. Would Matty ever forgive her? Would God ever forgive her? Dimly through the questions in her head she heard the radio.

'A man who's been helping police with their enquiries into a number of assaults has now been charged with the rape of a forty-five year old woman in the Croxteth area . . .' Teresa knew who they meant, she knew the woman and the man. So it was true. Matty had done it. Now she had no husband and no friend. She reached for the radio and tried to turn the knob to switch it off but it went the wrong way and the words got louder. She pushed the radio as far away as she could until it fell to the floor.

She reached for her cardigan: she'd need it. Even on a nice day there was usually a wind on the river. Teresa liked the river. It was where she and Matty had done a lot of their courting. They'd gone backwards and forwards on the ferry. It was as good as a day out when you hadn't much money. They hadn't had much money then, but at least they'd had each other. She picked up the radio before she went out. She didn't want people finding her house in a mess.

When Matty eventually got into the house through the kitchen window the first thing he saw was the note on the mantelpiece. 'Dear Matty,' it said. 'It was on the radio that you'd been charged. I just can't live with what you've done. And I can't live with what I did, letting the police get you. May God forgive me . . .'

When they found Teresa it was too late to explain her mistake. By the time they had fished her body out of the river she'd been dead for twenty-four hours.

At last Sandra heard from the newspaper about the story

159

she had sent in. A man called McNally from the Jupiter News Agency rang up and made an appointment to come round. Sandra went across to enlist Karen's help.

'I just want someone to sit with me. With Pat and Terry being out.'

'She's only a student, you know,' said Damon.

'Yes, but she knows something about it. I just feel a bit nervy about a journalist.'

'I'll be glad to come,' said Karen. 'Very glad.'

Karen had only spoken the truth. She was very glad indeed to have an excuse to get out of the house for an hour or two. Anything to take her mind off thinking about Teresa's death. The news had fallen like a bombshell on the Grants: Sheila had withdrawn into agonies of grief and Bobby tormented himself with reproaches at not having done enough. Karen longed to help both of them, but this was between them. They were out of reach of any help she could offer, and staying in did no good. It was a relief when Sandra at least seemed to need her.

McNally began with flattery.

'It's nice after a hard morning to meet a couple of pretty girls like you.'

'Women,' said Karen. 'Girls go to school.'

'Whatever you say, love. Now then, this Cribbs-Baker, he's a powerful man?'

'That's why I sent in the story,' said Sandra. 'It's because he's powerful, people have kept quiet.'

'So he could afford a good libel lawyer?'

'What's that mean?'

'Well, the hospital won't comment, or Dr Hurrell.'

'You've been talking to Tony?'

'Tony, eh? You and him are on pretty good terms are you?'

'What's that to do with Cribbs-Baker?'

'What we want is the personal angle. I believe this is the house that was involved in a siege last year.'

'That's it, is it?' said Karen.

'That's what?'

'You're just looking for smut aren't you? "I visit siege house one year on." You're not interested in Sandra's story, are you?'

'Every story's got to have bit of human interest.'

'"Nurse in siege involved in hospital scandal,"' mimicked Karen. 'I can just see it. If I were you Sandra, I'd throw him out.'

Sandra got up. 'There's the door.'

'No need for this.'

'Isn't there? I was trying to right a wrong, and this is what you do with it.'

'I know when I'm not wanted.'

'Good. You've got something between your ears, then.'

'Thanks for your hospitality, I'm sure.'

When he'd gone, Sandra and Karen had a cup of tea to calm their nerves. Sandra was upset. 'I'm not going to get anywhere, am I?'

'Doesn't look like it,' said Karen.

'They had all the papers. Why wouldn't they use my story?'

'Maybe if Tony had backed you they would,' said Karen.

'He's thinking of his career. It's not what you know, it's who you know if you want to get on as a doctor.'

'Maybe there are more important things than getting on.'

'I suppose you're right. Only I don't want to blame him.'

'Miss him do you?'

'How could I when I see him at work every day?'

'You could . . .'

'Yes.'

Heather did her packing for the trip to Hong Kong with mixed feelings. This assignment was quite a feather in her cap and she was excited at the prospect, but she didn't relish the thought of leaving Nick. Now that he was around all the time it seemed very hard to imagine life without him. It was so nice to come back to his warmth and comfort and caring concern at the end of a day's work. It seemed a poor bargain to exchange that for an empty hotel room.

Not that the last few weeks had been all roses. Adam was a joy but Heather still didn't find her relationship with the other two altogether easy. Ruth made it very plain that she and her father had a close relationship and sometimes she succeeded in making Heather feel a bit of an outsider. Heather had to remind herself that this was only to be expected. After all, Ruth had known Nick a lot longer than she had. She was sure that things would get better in time.

And she couldn't help hoping that Scott wouldn't stay much longer. When she'd originally made her offer of open house she'd thought it was only for a few days, but now there were ominous signs that Scott was making himself more and more at home. Every day, more of his books and records and clothes appeared, until Heather despaired of her house ever being peaceful and orderly again.

She discovered one or two unexpected things about Nick as well. More than once she would wake up to find that he wasn't in bed next to her. One morning she went downstairs to investigate. She found him downstairs in the lounge, seated in a chair, just thinking.

'What's the matter?' she asked.

'Nothing. I was awake and I didn't want to disturb you.'

'How long have you been out of bed?'

'Not long. I wanted a cup of tea.'

Heather felt the teapot. 'It's cold.'

'Longer than I thought, then.' Nick picked up a sketch pad with a half-finished cartoon. 'What do you think?'

'It's good. You know I think your work's good. You really should try and sell it.'

'You know what I said. I do it for you.'

'Coming back to bed?'

'Not just now.'

'Has inspiration struck?'

'Something like that.'

'I'm going to miss you when I'm away.'

'It's mutual.'

Nick took Heather to the airport at the start of her trip and she clung to him for a long time before she went through to International Departures.

'Look after the house.'

'Look after yourself.'

'I'll ring you when I can.'

'I'll think about you.'

'When you can?'

'All the time.'

'I could always not go.'

'That wouldn't do you any good at work. I married a career woman and that's what I want. Off you go.'

'I'll make it up to you when I come back.'

'I'll make sure you do.'

Paul was preparing a leaflet to be handed out to explain the purpose of the road block Kathleen Monaghan's committee were organizing. He tried it out on Annabelle.

'How does this sound? "Is your child safe on the roads?"'

'What?'

'This leaflet. I told Kathleen I'd see to the paperwork. "Is your child safe on the roads? Do you let your children out on their own? Join a group of concerned parents who have decided to resort to direct action."'

'You can't do that, Paul. Direct action? You can't break the law, just when I'm in line for the bench. Just the kind of thing Kathleen Monaghan would think of.'

'But she's right. It's disgraceful the way people shoot along in their cars. Have they no legs?'

'What should they do?'

'They could walk of course. Or cycle.'

The next day Annabelle came back with a present for Paul. He was in the front garden when she drove up.

'Had a good shopping expedition?'

'Not bad. Have a look in the boot.'

Paul, ever the gentleman, came across. 'I'll give you a hand.'

'Thanks. It's a bit awkward.' She opened the car boot. Inside was a bicycle.

'Glad you took my advice,' said Paul. 'Cycling's good for you. Better than jogging.'

'It isn't for me.'

'Who then?'

'You.'

'Oh . . .'

'You don't look very pleased.'

'It's a bit of a shock, that's all.'

Paul's new bike made Harry Cross' day. Harry was a lifelong cyclist. Bikes were something he really knew a lot about, and Harry was not the type to hide his light under a bushel.

'Smart,' he said. 'Drop handlebars. Mind if I have a go?'

'If you like,' said Paul.

'I've never seen you with a bike before. Still, it's one of the things you don't forget, isn't it? Like swimming.'

'Yes,' said Paul.

He gripped the handlebars firmly, put his right foot on the peddle and pushed off.

'Going to cock on?' asked Harry. 'Told you it's something you never forget.'

'Just getting used to it,' said Paul. Still with one foot on the ground and one on the pedal he pushed harder, scooting off until he was out of sight round the end of the Close.

Only then did he feel safe with his secret: he'd never learned to ride a bike. But he'd no intention of telling Harry and Ralph that, or Annabelle either. He'd already decided what to do. He'd go out every day with this bike, find somewhere quiet and by one means or another master the thing. That way none of them would ever find out.

Only mastering the art of cycling wasn't as easy as all that, especially for someone of Paul's age. He went out each day, letting Annabelle believe it was for the exercise, and tried to get the secret of how to balance on two wheels. But it stayed a secret. Taking one foot off the ground was easy, it was when he lifted the second foot and aimed it at where the second pedal ought to be that things went wrong. Somehow his foot never found the pedal, and as he waved it around trying to make contact, the bike inexorably tipped over. It took all Paul's will-power not to give up.

It was Adam Black who came to the rescue. He was on his way to the Close one day when he saw Paul struggling and put two and two together.

'You can't ride it, can you?'

'Who says I can't?'

'I've been watching. Lots of people can't.'

'Really?'

'It's easy really. I'll teach you. Get on and I'll hold the saddle.'

Adam was about the only person Paul would have trusted with his secret. He'd been fond of him ever since they'd first met in the Close, and the fact that Paul had been the one on the spot when Adam had his accident had strengthened the bond.

'Thanks,' he said.

The more Harry saw Paul scooting his bike out of the Close the more his suspicions grew.

'Look at that,' he said to Ralph. 'If you ask me he doesn't know how to ride it.'

'Don't be daft, Harry. Everybody can ride a bike.'

'Tell you what, we'll have a little bet. Fifty pence that he can't.'

'All right. But how're we going to know?'

'We'll watch, won't we? You take first shift.'

They had to watch for quite some time: Paul was getting very adept at getting out of the Close when no one was around. Even Annabelle was impressed by all his early rising. Heartened by Adam, he was determined to persevere. Bit by bit he got the knack.

Unluckily for Harry, he got it when Ralph was on duty at the window.

'Quick, Harry. Quick. Come here,' said Ralph.

'What is it now?'

'Paul Collins. Look, he's riding.' Harry looked, and Ralph was right. There was Paul, both feet on the pedals, both hands on the handlebars, bottom firmly on the saddle, coming up the middle of the Close on his bike.

'He's got both feet off the ground,' said Ralph. 'That's fifty pence you owe me.'

Chapter Twelve

Teresa's funeral was Sheila's first outing in public since the rape. In a way it did her good. There was no question of not going, she had to pay her respects to Teresa and she was determined to put a good face on it, if only for the sake of Teresa's boys. Thinking of them pulled her together a bit. There were worse fates than rape. At least she was still alive, and she still had her family around her.

At Matty's request, the funeral was to be quiet so only Sheila and Bobby were going from the Grants, leaving Damon and Karen to look after Claire. Neither of them minded not going. They wouldn't have known what to say to Matty or the boys.

'Why did she do it?' Damon asked Karen. 'I get down sometimes, but killing yourself . . .'

'A girl at university did it last term. She took pills. They say she was hoping to be found in time. A cry for help.'

'D'you think that's what Teresa was hoping? That somebody on the ferry would have noticed?'

'I dunno. I think she'd just had enough.'

Bobby was still reproaching himself for what had happened. After all, he'd been the last person to see Teresa.

'I should have known,' he said. 'Why didn't I make her let me in?'

'How d'you think I feel?' said Sheila. 'My best friend and I'd no idea what she was going through.'

'You'd been through enough yourself.'

'That's not an excuse. I should have been able to help her more.'

'You did your best didn't you? You tried to help her. You parted friends.'

'I'll miss her, Bob. It seems like half my life's gone, too. All the things we did together.'

'I know, girl.'

'You think you're safe, you think all's going well and then suddenly it all blows up in your face.'

'Just got to do the best we can, haven't we?'

'Yes. Just stick by me Bob.'

'And you stick by me.'

It was a lovely service. Teresa's neighbours had clubbed together and sent a wreath, and there were flowers from old friends and from the cleaners at the school where Teresa had worked. In pride of place on top of the coffin were two wreaths: a huge floral cross from Matty, and a pink and white heart from Teresa's mother and the boys. Sheila was puzzled about why the boys had sent flowers with their grandmother and not with Matty: it didn't seem right. She found out why after the service when she had a word with Stephen, Teresa's eldest.

'I'm very sorry, Stephen,' she said.

'Yes.'

'How are the others?' Teresa's two younger sons were standing with their grandmother looking at the flowers.

'All right.'

'You'll be going back home now will you?'

'No.'

'Won't your dad want you at home?'

'He won't get the chance. We're going to live at my nan's.'

'D'you mean for ever? Leave your dad on his own?'

'He can look after himself.'

Sheila was shocked. 'I can understand if you're upset. There are bound to be hard feelings. But I'm sure in time . . .'

'My mum'll still be dead won't she? And he killed her.'

'You can't say that.'

'As good as. He could as well have held her head under

168

the water. He left her, didn't he, and then got mixed up with the police?'

Sheila had felt her fair share of anger against Matty, but this wasn't fair. 'He couldn't have known she'd do this.'

'I want nothing more to do with him.'

'Then he's got nobody.'

'Serve him right.'

Sheila was bewildered by his bitterness. 'Does your nan think the same?'

'Yes.'

'So . . . what about going back to the house now?'

'We're not going with him. My nan's laid something on at hers. You're welcome, if you like, you and Bobby, so long as he doesn't come.'

Sheila hadn't yet dared look at Matty. She'd been aware of him walking down behind the coffin but she'd dropped her head and averted her eyes, partly to hide her tears but partly, too, to avoid seeing him. She'd never forget some of the awful things he'd said to her. But now she turned her head and searched him out.

He was standing a few yards away. This was the first time Sheila had seen him since she'd got out of the taxi on that dreadful night. Then he'd been angry and powerful and frightening; now he was sad, desolate and broken. Seeing him like that Sheila could no longer hate him, she could only feel sorry for him. The thought that he had to go from here on his own to an empty house, with no wife, no children, was more than she could bear. She walked across and held her arms out.

'Matty.'

Matty looked at her uncertainly, his face white.

'I've been talking to the family,' she said.

Matty's face flushed and he blinked his eyes. 'Yes.'

Sheila reached out a free hand to take Bobby's. 'We can't leave you on your own.'

'No,' said Bobby. 'Come on you two.' He squeezed Sheila's hand, then let go of it to take Matty's other arm. 'No arguing, you're coming back with us.'

Matty looked across to where his sons and Teresa's mother stood. He lifted his hand and tried to wave but they made no move towards him. 'Come on,' said Bobby. 'Let them gawp.'

The first bit of the afternoon wasn't too difficult. There was Claire to see to, explanations to Damon and Karen, lunch to make. But when that was all over and they'd eaten, it was difficult to know what to do. Karen and Damon both disappeared and Bobby took Claire for a walk. But neither Sheila or Matty could face going out again; besides, they needed time together. There were things they had to clear up.

'What have I done?' asked Matty. 'How've I got myself in this mess? If it wasn't for me, this would never have happened.'

'No good blaming yourself.'

'I know I can never make it right with you, Sheila, but I want you to know how sorry I am for what I said.'

'And I want you to know . . . oh, what I did . . . I only meant for the best. I'm sorry too.'

'I loved Teresa, I know that now. But I couldn't stand the life we were leading. Her working to keep me, getting on each other's nerves.'

'She's out of it now.'

'Yes. If only we could go back. Do it different.'

'I wish that too. But there isn't any going back.'

'There's no future is there? Not for me.'

'You have to find something. That's what Teresa would want.'

'What?'

'What about going on with your education?'

'I wish I'd never gone to that class . . .'

'You mustn't throw away what you've learned. Neither of us should. We have to build on it, make something of it. Otherwise it's all waste.'

'I can't think about it. Not yet.'

'I'll ask you again.'

Sheila wouldn't let Matty go home on his own that

170

night. She insisted that he stayed, and Bobby insisted too. Whatever had happened over these last few weeks, Bobby and Sheila were agreed that they had to stand by Matty now. Above all, they had to make sure that he didn't do what Teresa had done.

Damon did his bit to show his support for Matty off his own bat. Later that week he was waiting at the door when Matty came back from the shops.

'Not a scrap of food in,' said Matty. 'And I fancied a walk. Look, Damon, your mum didn't need to send you round.'

'Nobody sent me round. I've come off me own bat to offer my condolences. Especially about the family.'

'I can understand their reasons, I suppose.'

'It's not fair to blame you. The police got it wrong. And Auntie Teresa was a grown woman. She shouldn't have done what she did.'

'You've got an old head on young shoulders.'

'I'm a dolite, too, aren't I? I know that doing nothing can get you down. That's why I've come round.'

'Oh yes?'

'We're going to paint your house. It could do with a lick of paint.' Damon looked at the front door. 'More than a lick if you ask me.'

'You don't have to do this, lad.'

'I like decorating. It's what I'm good at. I only wish somebody'd pay me for doing it regular.'

'I wish I could.'

'No need. It's a present. For me Uncle Matty.'

Sheila had one more visit from Detective Sergeant Spencer. 'Sorry it's taken me so long to get round, but when someone's arrested and charged, there's a load of paperwork.'

'It didn't say who it was in the paper.'

'That's the law. In rape cases the victim and the defendant can't be identified by the press.'

Sheila didn't want to ask, and then again she did. She

was afraid to have a face, a name, a person to attach to what had been done to her, but not knowing seemed even worse. If she didn't know, it could be anybody, any man she saw. Until she knew she could never lay the matter to rest.

'Was it someone I've met?' She meant Ken Dinsdale.

'No. You've never seen him before and you'll never see him again.'

'Who?'

'It was the cabby. We caught him red-handed with another woman. The fourth; you were the third.'

'I'll never go in a taxi again. I suppose it was him who blamed Matty?'

'I'm afraid so.'

'Poor Teresa.'

'Anyway, all you've got to do is sign this deposition. Then you won't need to go to court.'

'Oh.' A great burden lifted from Sheila. 'That's a blessing.'

'The proceedings'll just be a formality. They'll sentence him, that's all.'

'So as far as I'm concerned, it's over?'

'Yes.'

When she'd gone, Sheila turned to Bobby. 'Hold me, love.' It was the first time she'd asked that. Bobby held his arms wide, then wrapped them round her.

'It's over, love. It's definitely over.'

Annabelle got a letter inviting her to an interview with the Clerk to the Justices, a Mr Jack Nelson. It couldn't have been worse timed: the appointment was the day after the road block Kathleen Monaghan had planned. Just before Annabelle went for an interview that might make her a Justice of the Peace, her own husband intended to break the law.

Not that that was how Paul saw it. 'I'm involved in a demonstration to highlight a road safety hazard, not robbing a bank.'

172

'You're deliberately breaking the law. It's the same thing.'

'Actually, I've thought of a way of keeping within the law.'

'How?'

'We'll all keep moving.'

'Will that make it all right?'

'Nobody can stop us crossing the road. It's just that with a lot of us we'll do it nonstop.'

'There must be a law against it.'

Paul was smug. 'If you think crossing the road can be an illegal act, are you sure you're fit to be a magistrate?'

But when the time came Paul's strategy didn't stop the police taking an interest in what was going on. Paul and Kathleen were organizing their troops, who consisted entirely of women and children, when a constable approached them. 'Are you the organizer?' he asked Paul.

'We both are,' said Kathleen.

'Do you realize that it's an offence to stop the traffic? If that's what you intend to do.'

'We have to cause a disruption, or nothing'll happen,' said Kathleen.

'And we don't mean to break the law,' said Paul.

'It's my job to keep the traffic moving.'

'Just understand you work for us as well as them with cars,' said Kathleen.

'I don't need you to tell me what my job is.'

'It's to make sure none of the drivers run us residents down.'

'Shall we start?' said Paul.

'Yes.'

Paul raised his arm and everyone looked at him expectantly. He hadn't felt as good as this since the day he'd been made redundant: he hadn't realized quite how much he missed having things to organize and people who did what he told them to. 'Are you ready?' he said. He paused to savour the moment, and then lowered his hand.

'Go.'

Two of the women stepped forward and after them two more.

'All right,' said the policeman, 'Two can play at that game.' And he unclipped his radio phone.

Kathleen had arranged that the man from the local paper should report the demo. The photographer was in the middle of taking some pictures of a particularly attractive toddler and his even more attractive mother when the constable's reinforcements arrived. The police driver didn't waste much time. 'Would you like to step in here,' he said to Paul, holding the car door invitingly open.

'No, I would not. Can't you see I'm busy?' said Paul.

'Well in that case,' said the driver, 'I'm afraid I must insist.' And he took Paul firmly by the arm. The photographer turned round. He was just in time to take a clear close-up of Paul Collins being taken into police custody.

It was printed right in the middle of the front page of the local paper the next day, with Paul's name and address underneath it, plain for all to see.

Under the circumstances Annabelle didn't think it was really worthwhile keeping the appointment with Jack Nelson. But she wasn't the kind of person who let people down. Besides she'd had her hair done and bought a pair of new shoes in honour of the occasion, so she thought she might as well. On the way, she tried to work out what the best tactic would be if she were asked about Paul and his behaviour. Perhaps she could make a joke of it. 'My husband, yes . . . I'm married to an anarchist.' Even if Mr Nelson wouldn't be able to see the joke Annabelle could, and she'd cheered up a bit by the time she arrived.

Jack Nelson was a very pleasant surprise. He was tall, good-looking, well dressed and charming.

'Are you nervous?' he asked her.

'Trying not to be.'

'There's no need. This is just an informal chat to make sure you haven't got two heads or anything.'

'No, just the one.' Annabelle decided it would be very nice to work with this man.

'Silly question really, but was it your husband I saw in the paper this morning?'

'I'm afraid so.'

'Why afraid? I'd've thought you would be proud of him.'

'Oh, yes.' Annabelle had never realized before how well she could pretend.

'It's good to see people caring for their community.'

'Dortmund Way isn't really our community. We are some distance away.'

'All the better then. Being public-spirited must run in the family. Him doing that and you applying here.'

'I hadn't thought of it like that.'

'Now, down to business. You've been a teacher haven't you?'

'Yes.'

'So you've some idea about how to handle young people?'

'I hope so. Is it important?'

'Understanding people is. We get all sorts up in Court. Are you in touch with what goes on around you?'

'Well, I read the local press.'

'It's been downhill all the way in Liverpool since the heady days of the sixties. A bit like the morning after a good party, when you're left with the mess.'

'Lack of money doesn't help.'

'No. And somebody has to pick up the pieces. Do you think you could help with that?'

Annabelle decided she liked Jack and it was fairly clear that he liked her. By the time he began to explain what would happen next, she was beginning to be hopeful. 'If you're accepted you'll start training. And sit with some experienced magistrates to get the feel of the job.' She left with a fairly clear impression that she would be selected.

Not even getting home to find Kathleen Monaghan

ensconced in her lounge having a post mortem with Paul could dampen her euphoria.

'How did you get on?' asked Paul.

'Very well. Very well indeed.'

'D'you think they'll have you then?'

'They're going to let me know. But I think so.'

Kathleen was doubtful. 'I hope you'll not want to make an example of decent young kids,' she said.

'I hope I'll be fair.'

'There's fair and fair, isn't there?'

'Stealing's stealing, isn't it?'

'It's not always that simple though, is it? Last Christmas a kid near us got community service for pinching a bike. Now his dad'd disappeared and his mum's no money so he couldn't have one. I know he shouldn't have done it, but d'you think he deserves having a record? What chance in life has he got now? Think of that when you're up there laying the law down.'

Tracy Corkhill was enjoying the summer holidays. She liked staying in bed late and then having plenty of time to doll herself up before she went round to her friends to listen to records or just mooch about. She didn't mind how long that kind of life went on; which was just as well since she was sixteen in the middle of August and, like Rod, she'd now left school.

Unlike Rod, she had no qualifications and no particular ambition either. She knew she had very little chance of getting a job, and she'd no intention of wasting too much time looking. The sort of jobs she might have been eligible for were far too boring to suit Tracy.

But although Tracy enjoyed this hanging around Doreen didn't.

'Can't you find something better to do than comb your hair and read magazines all day?'

'Such as?'

'Help me, for one thing.'

'Ar, eh mam, I was going to go round to Tina's.'

'In your dressing gown?'

'No, in me new skirt.'

'Can't you think about anything except clothes?'

Obviously Tracy couldn't. She'd spotted something in the magazine. 'Look at this evening dress. Off the shoulder and diamante trimmings.'

Naturally, it was Tracy who suggested that Doreen should hold a clothes party. 'Julie's mum has them,' she said. 'You get people round, show them the clothes, and you get a percentage of what they spend.'

'Why should I want to do that?'

'You were just saying how fed up you are stopping in on your own whilst now me dad's always out at work. If you had a clothes party you wouldn't be on your own.'

'This is all for my sake is it?'

Tracy looked innocent. 'I don't know what you mean.'

'Oh don't you. What about somebody not too far away from me who gets to try out the latest fashions? And then cons her mother into buying her something.'

'I won't ask you to buy any, honest mum. It'd be good though, wouldn't it? Better than sitting at home on our own.'

'Oh, all right, you win. Just so long as you help get the house clean.'

Tracy jumped up and hugged her mother. 'Oh I will. You're a lovely mum.'

Doreen decided to ask the women she worked with and some of the neighbours. Billy was doubtful.

'I can't see Annabelle Collins coming to buy catalogue seconds.'

'They're not seconds. They're end-of-season bargains.'

'And returns. I bet half the town's worn them at one time and sent them back.'

'They haven't. And don't go saying that in front of the customers.'

Julia Brogan, Doreen's mother, was nearly as thrilled as Tracy at the thought of the clothes party. 'I'll come early and help you,' she said. 'We'll get a few drinks in.'

'I was only thinking of tea and coffee.'

'You want more than that,' said Julia. 'You want to be hospitable.'

'We're doing this to make money, not spend it.'

'Get them a bit merry and they'll spend more, won't they? Come on, give me your list and I'll get off and do the shopping.'

'Make sure you stick to the list and all.'

'I'm a free spirit, I like to wander round the aisles and fill me basket as the spirit takes me.'

'Get some draught wine from the off licence, red and white, it's cheaper. And half a bottle of whisky for Billy.'

By the time Julia came back from the shops, the half bottle of whisky had become a whole one, and there were four bottles of wine. Doreen protested, but it was like water off a duck's back to Julia.

'Two bottles looked nothing. You'll not get people to spend with that. People'll need more.'

'You mean you will.'

'I know how to get a party going.'

Tracy didn't need any of the wine to get her going. She spent half the afternoon getting ready, and was standing there ready to hand down biscuits when the first guest arrived. Julia sidled across to her. 'You go round with them, give them a thirst, then I'll follow with the drinks.'

'All right.'

'Just keep handing them round, whatever your mum says. We don't want people to think we're stingy, do we?'

But Tracy didn't have much time to do what Julia said. She'd only just started on her first round when Jackie, the party organizer, spotted her.

'Is that your Tracy?' she said to Doreen.

'Yes.'

'She has grown up, hasn't she? D'you think she'd do the modelling for us tonight?'

'What's that mean?'

178

'The clothes look much better worn than just on the hangers, so we generally try and find somebody who'll try them on. She looks just the right size.'

'Ask her.'

Tracy was delighted to accept. 'Just like Hollywood,' she said. 'From waitress to model in two minutes.'

All this was too much for Billy. For once, all the machines he was supposed to be maintaining seemed to be behaving themselves and he wasn't going to waste one of his few free evenings at the clothes party surrounded by women. As Tracy set off upstairs to look at the clothes she was to wear he set off for the pub. In the Close he saw Bobby Grant.

'Bedlam in there,' he said. 'I'm going for a bevvy. Do you fancy one?'

'I would,' said Bobby, 'but I'm baby-sitting. Making do with a few cans.'

'Fancy some company?'

'I do. But I've only got four cans.'

'Don't let that bother you,' said Billy. 'I've got some Scotch I can bring. Any other husbands need a refuge?'

'Paul Collins might. If Annabelle's going to yours.'

'Let's ask him.'

The clothes party was going well. Tracy enjoyed herself modelling the clothes and Julia enjoyed pouring out the drinks, and between them business was brisk. Jackie was delighted. 'Just give me your orders. No need to pay till you get what you want, so you've plenty of time to get round your husbands.'

Tracy smiled at her mother. 'Told you this was a good idea.'

The party at the Grants' was going well, too. They'd got through Bobby's cans of ale and were well on their way through Billy's bottle of whisky. Bobby was teaching them poker. The fact that they were only playing for tenpence stakes didn't stop the excitement rising high. Billy's nerve broke first. 'I'll pack,' he said.

'Sevens and fours,' said Paul.

'Jacks and nines,' said Billy with delight. 'It's mine.'

'Best party I've done this year,' said Jackie.

'Thanks to the wine,' said Julia.

'And Tracy,' said Doreen.

'I could do with taking her round with me,' said Jackie. She's got a flair for modelling. Would you like that?'

'She'd be in her glory,' said Doreen.

'Would you let me, mum?'

'Well . . .' Doreen hesitated.

'Please, mum. I'll do all your dusting.'

'Since you ask.'

'Please, mum.'

'I suppose anything's better than just hanging around.'

And Doreen got another hearty hug.

Chapter Thirteen

At the end of his month's suspension, Bobby went back to work with very mixed feelings. He was glad to have something to do again, but the fact that he'd been out-manoeuvred over the business at Bragg's had knocked the stuffing out of him. In his absence, George had got the men back to work with no improvement in their differentials and with nothing to show for the strike except three weeks' loss of pay. If being district secretary meant letting people down like that, Bobby wasn't sure he wanted to know any more.

He couldn't resist referring to the matter on his first day back. 'Have you got the job yet, George?'

'What job?'

'You know, the national job. Your reward for toeing the nice safe line at Bragg's.'

'Give it a rest will ya.'

'So what's happened?'

'Nothing's happened. If you must know it's looking as if it might go to somebody else.'

That didn't make Bobby feel any better. It seemed that George had sold the men at Bragg's down the river for nothing. And there was nothing Bobby could do about it, not without risking his job. The way he felt at the moment he might even have done that if it hadn't been for Sheila and Claire.

A man poked his head round the office door. ' 'Scuse me,' he said.

'Hang on a minute,' said George.

'Who's that?' asked Bobby.

'Billy Preece. Industrial injury.'

Bobby felt uncomfortable. 'We aren't management you know, George. We're here to talk to the workers, not keep them waiting.'

'See him if you want,' said George. 'But I warn you he's trying it on. He's made a load of claims before. You know the kind.'

Bobby did. It wasn't unknown for people working with dangerous substances to hurt themselves deliberately so as to get compensation. He knew one or two who'd had a decent holiday doing something like that.

He raised it with Preece. 'What about all these previous claims you've made?'

'You work with acid, you get burnt. If you followed all the safety warning, you'd never get your bonus.'

'Your last claim was turned down on the basis it was self-inflicted.'

'Same old line, eh. Last time I made a claim, George Williams talked like you. Just like management . . . whose side are you on?' He stood up and lifted his shirt. On his back there was a livid burn. 'Self-inflicted, that? Would anybody in their right mind do that on purpose? Me wife says I should leave, but where else am I gonna get a job at my age?'

Bobby was persuaded. 'Right,' he said. 'Just let me get me pen and I'll take the details.'

'You mean you'll back me?' said Preece.

'Of course I'll back you. It's what we're here for isn't it?' Bobby settled firmly in his chair. He may have lost a battle but he hadn't lost the war. This was the kind of thing he'd taken this job for, to help men like Preece. It was still worth doing after all. It was nice to be back to normal after all that had happened.

Sheila wished for nothing so much as that things could be normal. But it was increasingly clear that they weren't. She could only bury her head in the sand for so long, and that time had run out. She had to face the fact that her period was two weeks late.

She looked at the calendar in her hand and counted the days again in the hope she might be wrong. But there was no doubt: today was the fourteenth day.

She let her fear become concrete. All these years she'd been regular. When she had been late there had only ever been one reason: that she was pregnant.

She curled up on the bed, weak with the horror of really facing it. There couldn't be any doubt about how this had come about. It was over a year now since Bobby had had his vasectomy so the baby wasn't his. And there'd only been one other man, the man who'd attacked her by the dark roadside: the rapist. This was a rapist's child.

Sheila felt sick and terrified. It seemed unbearably cruel that this should happen, just when they'd thought they could put the awful events of the last month behind them. Now they never could. Sheila knew quite clearly even in the middle of all her fear and dread that she could never kill this baby.

That wasn't Bobby's view when she told him. 'You couldn't possibly think about having it,' he said. 'If you do this'll never be over. Get rid of it.'

'It! We're talking about human life.'

'How can you say that? It isn't a person, not yet. It's no bigger than a pinhead.'

'Like our Claire was?'

'You can't compare. She's ours. We love each other. This wasn't started in love, it was started in violence. Hate. The church will have to be flexible on this.'

'It isn't the church saying no, Bob, it's me. My conscience. I can't get rid of it.'

It was impossible to hide what was going on from Karen. Over these last few weeks she'd grown closer to her mother, protective and aware of her moods. She half heard what they were talking about, and quickly picked up what was the matter.

'You're pregnant, aren't you?'

'Yes.'

'You're not going to have it?'

'Leave me alone, can't you? You're as bad as your dad.'

'If you do, it'll remind you. For ever.'

Sheila was distressed but sure. 'I can't stop it. I just can't.'

Karen and Bobby talked together. 'D'you think she'd listen to the priest?' suggested Karen.

'The way she is now we'd need the Pope at least.'

'Perhaps she blames herself for Teresa's death. She might be wanting to punish herself.'

'It won't just affect her though, will it?' said Bobby. 'We'll all suffer. It's not right what she's doing.'

'No,' said Karen. 'But she'll take some persuading.'

'I wish you could persuade her, girl. Doesn't look as if I can.'

Karen did her best. She waited till she had Sheila on her own and started. 'I like this family, mum.'

'That's a funny thing to say.'

'It's true. I love all of you. My dad, even when he doesn't understand, our Barry, Damon even when he's daft, and our Claire.'

'What are you trying to say?'

'That I love you. You're the best mother anybody could have. But you're not being fair to us now.'

'I didn't want for this to happen.'

'But you have a choice whether it goes on. You can stop it.'

Sheila was silent. She felt very alone. She didn't know what she would have done without Bobby and Karen's support these last few weeks, but now she and they were on opposite sides. She made one more attempt to make Karen understand. 'It's just an idea to you, this baby. But to me it's real, as real as any of you. It's the same as when you started, or our Barry, or Damon, or Claire. I can't kill it.'

'What about us? Will you put us all through it for years just because you got in the wrong taxi? And you've got to think about your age. Don't you realize it's dangerous? It might be handicapped.'

184

'Don't go on, Karen. I know you don't understand. Perhaps I am wrong and it's you that's right, but that doesn't change anything. To me it's life, and I have to look after it. I can't argue about it, it's something I feel.'

Karen and Bobby put their heads together. 'What about ringing Auntie Margaret?' asked Karen. 'D'you think she might talk her round?'

'I don't know. What if she agrees with your mum?'

'How can she? It's a rapist's baby?'

'I wish I could just rip the thing away from her. I don't think I can watch it grow, see it born. And I couldn't bring it up. It'd take a bigger man than I am to do that.'

Sheila kept herself busy all day: shopping, cooking, cleaning. She kept as far away from Karen and Bobby as she could. They didn't start trying to persuade her again, but she heard them whispering together, and she saw the glances they exchanged, and the way they watched her. She was at rock bottom. She knew they thought she was wrong, she felt very alone, she didn't know where to turn for help.

Yet in another way she felt very strong. Now that her principles were so cruelly tested she knew clearly where she stood. She'd do what she thought was right no matter what it cost her. She was sad that Karen and Bobby seemed to think she was being selfish, when to her it didn't feel like that at all. Going ahead with this pregnancy seemed very hard, but she knew she had to do it if she wasn't to betray her deepest convictions. That day Sheila prayed for strength as she'd never prayed before.

She dozed fitfully all night and woke in the morning with a feeling of heaviness and dread. She lay for a moment, weary to death and with an ache in her back. It was only when she shifted to try and ease the ache that she realized this was something she'd felt often before. Half hoping, half fearing, she checked: what she hoped was true. Her period had started.

Bobby was ecstatic. 'That's wonderful, girl,' he said.

185

'Better late than never. I've never been so glad in my life.'

'Sure you feel all right now? D'you want a cup of tea fetching up?'

Sheila laughed for what seemed the first time in weeks. 'No need for that, I'm not an invalid. Everything's back to normal. I'm perfectly all right.'

Although Nick was missing Heather, he wasn't exactly lonely. For a start, he had Scott for company and in some ways that was easier with Heather away. Nick was by nature more tolerant than Heather, and more used to children. Besides, Scott was his own and he was glad to have more opportunity to spend time with him.

Ruth dropped in quite a lot, too, though Nick was never quite sure whether the main attraction as far as she was concerned was him or Rod Corkhill. He still wasn't very happy about that relationship but there wasn't much he could do about it. With Ruth still on holiday from school and Rod at home waiting to hear the result of his job application, they had plenty of opportunity to meet whilst Nick was in reluctant attendance at the city architects' office.

On one particular day, Nick was downright relieved that Heather was safely on the other side of the world. He and Scott were in the middle of breakfast when there was a knock on the door. Scott went to answer it.

'It's Charlie,' he called.

'Let him in, then.'

Charlie inspected Scott's cornflakes. 'It's years since I had them,' he said. 'Got any milk, Nick?'

Nick fetched another bottle from the fridge. 'What brings you here so early?' he asked.

'I've come from the flat.'

'Your flat or mine?'

'Yours, of course. I wouldn't call my bedsit a flat. I'd been at a party at the uni, and I thought I'd crash out at your place seeing it was half past four. Nearer you see.'

'And you're up at this time?'

'There's a reason for that.' Charlie looked warningly towards Scott. 'You've had visitors.'

Nick was anxious. 'What kind of visitors?'

'Not . . . I mean burglars.'

'Did they get anything?'

'They were only looking for money, I think. It's all right.'

'You should get the police,' said Scott.

'No need,' said Nick.

'Oh, go on, dad.'

'You heard,' Nick was suddenly sharp. 'We don't want the police. Do we, Charlie?'

'We don't,' said Charlie. 'Better not to bother. Still, we don't want this to happen again, do we?'

'What's this about?' asked Nick.

'Me staying at your flat. Things are getting a bit heavy at my place.'

'How heavy?'

'I owe three months rent. I tried to work the charm bit, but it didn't work.'

'I suppose you think the charm'll work with me?'

'Why not? It always has, hasn't it?'

But Charlie was in no hurry to move into the flat: Charlie was rarely in much of a hurry about anything. He was still at Heather's when the last bus went, and by then Nick was in no state to give him a lift.

'Might as well crash here, then,' said Charlie.

'This is Heather's house,' said Nick.

'Yours, now. And when she's away the boys will play.'

'Just tonight, then.'

Charlie was just getting up when Ruth called round the next morning. She wasn't very pleased to see him.

'What's he doing here?' she said to Nick.

'He stayed late, so he slept here.'

'He's moving into dad's flat,' said Scott.

Ruth looked at her father with exasperation. 'D'you never learn?' she said. 'Why do you let him rip you off?'

'He's my oldest friend.'

'He's no good for you. You shouldn't let him get away with it. He won't pay you any rent for the flat, you know.'

'He will. He's got some lecturing coming up.'

'Always something coming up, isn't there? Only it's never today, always tomorrow.'

'There's no need to be rude, it's my business. Just remember you're my daughter, not my wife.'

'Heather wouldn't like it.'

'Heather's not here is she?'

The close encounter with the police didn't discourage Paul in his effort to get a crossing in Dortmund Way. On the contrary it made him more determined than ever. He and Annabelle had quite a few useful contacts in high places, and by making a few phone calls and mentioning a few names, he was able to arrange for some councillors and a representative of the local authority to make a visit to the proposed site rather sooner than they might have done had the paperwork gone through the usual channels. Kathleen was pleased and impressed, but that didn't stop her carrying on in her usual manner.

'I don't know why we don't already have a crossing on this road,' she said to the councillors who came on the visit. 'There's lorries as well as cars go along here with no respect for speed limits or nothing. You should have done something about it long since.'

'We do have other duties, Mrs Monaghan.'

'More important than saving children's lives?'

Paul decided it was time he took a grip on things. 'Shall we look at the place we're suggesting?' he said.

'There's two,' said Kathleen. 'We'll look at them both.'

This was the first Paul had heard of a second suggestion, but he didn't want to get involved in an argument. 'This is where I was thinking of,' he said. 'Plenty of visibility for motorists.'

'But it's not the nearest for the primary school kids,'
188

said Kathleen. 'They'll have to walk all the way from Latters Road and back again. What we need is two crossings. One down here and one up there.'

Paul wished Kathleen would shut up. She was asking for the moon. They'd be lucky to get one crossing; there was no chance of two. Councillor Lodge, the husband of a friend of Annabelle's, said as much to Paul as they followed Kathleen down the road. 'You've got to shut her up. Two crossings is a no-hoper. Go for one and we can probably help.'

'Is there a real chance, then?'

'Luck's on your side. There's a bye-election in this ward.'

'How will that help?'

'Best chance of getting anything done is at election time. Our candidate'll support the crossing, and so the other one'll have to . . . he couldn't risk seeming not to care about children. It'll be an issue.'

'So we've got a reasonable chance?'

'A good one.'

Paul shook his hand on it. 'Thanks, Steven.'

Kathleen was cock-a-hoop when the visiting party had gone. 'Looks like we've won.'

'Why did you suddenly talk about two crossings?'

'You're not the only one knows your way around you know. I've done this before.'

'It didn't look like it.'

'It's tactics to ask for twice as much as you need. That way they think they're meeting you halfway. We don't need two crossings, just one. Looks like we've got it and all.'

In the end, Pat had to admit that Terry was right: things were over between him and Sandra. These days he hardly saw anything of her. She ate at the hospital, worked extra hours whenever she could, and even when she was at home she shut herself away upstairs. Now that he'd accepted that the relationship was over, Pat was glad she

189

kept out of his way. It was seeing her that hurt; when she wasn't around to remind him of what had been, he could at least make a start on trying to forget.

He didn't feel so bad when the van business was busy. Pat enjoyed driving and meeting different people, and the physical labour of humping things up and down stairs made him feel healthily tired. Unfortunately there wasn't really enough work to provide two people with a full-time job. He and Terry spent quite a lot of time hanging about waiting for the phone to go.

The start of the football season gave Terry an idea for using this enforced leisure constructively. 'What about going down the football club, do a bit of training?'

'No,' said Pat. 'My idea of exercise is lying on a hot beach.'

'You're in the wrong place for that.'

'I'll come and watch. I suppose it can't be worse than just sitting waiting for the phone to ring. But I'm not training.'

Whilst Terry was changing, Pat found himself a sheltered spot and took his shirt off to catch the warmth from the sun. He shifted a bit to keep out of the wind and closed his eyes. If he tried very hard, perhaps he could pretend he was on some foreign beach. He imagined that the shouts he could hear weren't Terry and his mates hitting a ball about, but bikini-clad girls running into the sea. It was the nearest he'd get to the real thing. On the money they were making, the closest he'd been to a holiday this year was a day or two on the beach at Formby. Pat lay back and let his imagination run riot.

When he opened his eyes he thought he was still imagining things. There was a woman by the side of him, and what a woman. She was expensively dressed, she smelt marvellous and she looked gorgeous. And she was sitting next to him. And talking to him. As if she wanted to.

'Hi,' she said. 'I'm Andrea.'

'Pat.'

190

'Pleased to meet you.'

'And me.' That was an understatement.

'D'you think it's warm enough to take my shirt off?'

Pat gulped. 'I have.'

'Good.' Andrea unbuttoned her blouse to reveal that under it she was wearing a bikini top. Pat couldn't believe his luck. This was a lot better than football.

'You're not training?' she asked.

'Not today,' said Pat. He guessed she'd like a sporty type and rubbed his leg. 'I've had a bit of an injury. Just giving it a rest.'

'I thought I hadn't seen you around.'

'D'you come here often?'

'Oh yes. Every home game and most aways.' Pat was beginning to think that Terry had had a good idea, coming down to the club. He could see that he could become very interested in football after all.

Andrea was stretching out on the grass. Pat sat up to watch her. 'I like the sun, don't you?' she said. 'My idea of a holiday is sun and sand.'

'Nice when you can get it,' said Pat.

'D'you do weight training?' asked Andrea. She was looking at Pat with an admiration that was making him feel better than he'd felt for weeks.

'No.'

'You're very fit then.'

'We've got a removal business. You need muscles for carrying stuff about.'

'We're in business too,' she said. 'Me and my husband.'

So she had a husband. Of course it had been too good to be true. There was no way a woman like this could be available even if she did seem to be sending out signals that she was. 'Married, are you?' he said, as casually as he could.

'Yes. Twelve years. But I don't let it stop me having fun.'

'You don't look old enough.'

'Well, I started young. You married?'

'No.'

'Don't tell me there's nobody making an offer for you.'

Pat wondered how much to say. He didn't want Andrea to think he wasn't in demand, but he wanted to make it plain he wasn't spoken for somewhere. 'There was somebody,' he said. 'But we've just broken up.' It hurt him again, saying it like that, but Andrea's response helped quite a lot.

'I'm in luck then, aren't I?' she said. 'Though I can't believe any girl in her right mind'd let you go.'

There was no way Pat was going to leave things there. If the way to see Andrea again was to play football, then he'd play football. He broached the subject with Terry.

'Who do I see if I want to get on the team?'

'I thought you didn't want to know?'

'That was before.'

'Before what?'

'When you were training I changed my mind.'

'Why?'

'I met this gorgeous woman. She goes down and watches a lot. Honestly, Terry, I'd do more than play footy for her.'

'Blonde?'

'Yes.'

'Terrific figure?'

'Yes.'

'Clothes so tight you can see her breathing?'

'How do you know all this?'

'What's her name?'

'Andrea.'

'Oh no.'

'What d'you mean, "Oh no." '

'D'you know she's married?'

'As a matter of fact she told me.'

'Did she tell you who to?'

'I didn't ask.'

'Well, she married to Bernie Parkin. Club manager and

192

a lot more besides. Some of his friends are a bit on the rough side. She's a man-eater, Pat, keep out of her way. She's spat bigger blokes than you out in little pieces.'

'What have I to lose?'

'Your good health for a start.'

Pat wasn't going to be frightened off that easily. 'Maybe it's worth taking a bit of a risk to have a bit of life. What else is there for me?'

'A big risk.'

'That's my choice, isn't it? I'll take whatever I have the chance to take. I'm not scared of Bernie Parkin.'

The Collins had a letter from their son Gordon. Annabelle recognized the handwriting when she picked it off the mat. 'A letter from France,' she said to Paul.

'Lucy?'

'No, Gordon.'

'What does he have to say?'

Annabelle skimmed it quickly. 'Well, this is a surprise.'

'Are you going to tell me?'

'He wants to come home.'

'That *is* a surprise.'

'With a friend.'

'What kind of friend?'

Annabelle knew what Paul meant. 'He doesn't say.'

'We'll have to wait and find out then.'

'Shall I write and say yes?'

'Of course. After all, he is our son. No matter what. And we're all a bit older and wiser, aren't we?'

It was nearly two years now since Gordon had left home. He'd gone very suddenly and some of the hurt was still there. He'd been only sixteen at the time, studying for his O levels at an independent school. It hadn't been easy for them to find the fees, but they'd been determined to give Gordon the best start in life. So it had come as a particularly cruel blow when he'd thrown it all away.

Annabelle had come in one day to find Gordon gone,

and only a note to explain why. She'd never forget what it said: 'I'm going to look round for a while. I'm sorry. I've borrowed forty quid, but that with my savings will keep me going. I'll see you when I've grown up, but I'll have to get away for it to happen. I'm sorry if it upsets you.'

There was no more explanation. They had no idea what had led him to take such an action.

When they found out it had been an even greater shock. A Mrs Duncan had called to see Annabelle unexpectedly, and in a state of great distress. Her distress was about her son Christopher, head boy at Gordon's school. 'What's he to do with Gordon?' Annabelle had asked.

'Hasn't Gordon mentioned him?'

'No.'

'So you don't know?'

'Don't know what?'

'Christopher and Gordon. Christopher told us, Mrs Collins, that he's homosexual.'

'Yes?'

'And he and Gordon . . . they were very close.'

'You don't mean . . .?'

'Yes. I believe they've recently quarrelled. Over a girl.'

'Kathy?'

'Yes.' This couldn't be true. Kathy was Gordon's girlfriend, wasn't she? But Mrs Duncan was carrying on.

'I think Gordon was trying to prove something by seeing her. And when Christopher suggested as much, Gordon broke off with him. But then he found that Christopher was right.'

Annabel hoped that what she was thinking was wrong. 'What do you mean?'

'I think you know what I mean, Mrs Collins. Christopher and Gordon were very special friends. More than friends.'

And that was the first the Collins knew about their son being involved in a homosexual relationship.

*

Paul finished reading the letter from France.

'This friend,' he said. 'He doesn't say . . .'

'I'm sure he'd let us know if there were any . . . complications.' They both knew what she meant.

'I hope you're right. Perhaps he's grown out of it.'

'What if he hasn't? If his friend is his . . . lover . . do we put them in the same room?'

'I couldn't allow that. And I'm sure Gordon wouldn't expect it.'

'Let's just hope the friend's a girl.'

Chapter Fourteen

The first thing Guy did when he came back to Liverpool at the end of the summer holidays was to drive to Brookside to see Karen. He'd been abroad for most of the summer and he'd missed her a lot.

'It's really good to see you again,' he said.

'Me too.'

'Letters aren't the same are they?'

'No, they're not.' And yet in a way it had been easier for Karen that Guy had been away. The attack on Sheila and its aftermath had drawn the family close together, and maybe Guy wouldn't have had a place in all that. Karen had told him that Sheila hadn't been well but she hadn't explained why. The fact that her mother had been raped seemed too private to share in a letter.

Now that Guy was back, the problem of somewhere to live had to be solved quickly. Guy had given up his room in hall at the end of the summer term so now he was homeless. The problem wasn't instant: Bobby had taken a couple of weeks' holiday and gone away with Sheila and Claire for a much-needed change of scene, and whilst her parents were away Karen could have Guy to stay in Brookside Close. But that couldn't go on when they came home.

So it was time to go flat-hunting in earnest. Karen decided to look first and tell her parents afterwards. Her anxiety about what her mother would say about the plan to live with Guy hadn't gone away – if anything the awful events of this summer made it worse. Karen had a shrewd suspicion that her mother wasn't going to take at all kindly to the idea of her leaving home.

But for the moment Guy's enthusiastic flat-hunting stilled her doubts. He looked in the local papers every day and made endless phone calls, until eventually he found somewhere in Wavertree at a price they could afford. He wanted Karen to look at it at once.

'I can't go today,' she said. 'I've got a job, don't forget. I've got to be on Ainsdale Beach selling ice creams.'

'We'll take the van with us and set up shop there. Kids in Wavertree like ice cream too, you know.'

'I hope they do. If my takings go down you'll be in trouble.'

'They'll go up with my sales talk.'

'Well, I suppose it's worked on me.'

The flat, when they found it, was three rooms in a big old house. It wasn't wonderful but it wasn't terrible either. Guy was all in favour and Karen couldn't think of any objections, so they agreed to take it. What's more, the children in Wavertree bought ice cream with enthusiasm. Karen and Guy arrived back in Brookside Close with Guy at least in high spirits.

'We're householders *and* we sold out of ice cream,' he said. 'Just think of the commission.'

'We're going to need it to afford that flat.'

'Sure you're happy about it, Karen?'

Karen decided to come clean.

'I am. But I'm not sure my mum will be.'

'You can't still be having to ask her permission.'

'It's not that easy. She's had a hard time this summer.'

'Being ill?'

'It was worse than that. She was raped.'

Guy was shocked. 'Oh no. That's terrible.'

'It's left her a bit nervy. So I don't want to spring anything on her.'

'I can see that. But what about me? It's not just because I want someone to cook, to keep me warm, you know. You matter to me, Karen.'

'I know. I feel the same about you. Only we can't rush things.'

'She seemed to get used to the idea of you staying over sometimes last term.'

'Yes, and I'll still do that. Perhaps do it more often. That way she'll just find out gradually.'

'It's not what I want. But I see the point.'

'And it'll be lovely when I do stay.'

The flat was supposed to be let furnished, but the furniture in it was minimal: a battered bed, a wobbly chest of drawers and one chair. So when they passed a junk shop with a kitchen table and six chairs on display Guy couldn't resist stopping to buy them.

'How're we going to carry them?' asked Karen. 'D'you want me to have a word with Pat and Terry?'

'No need,' said Guy. 'What's wrong with that?' 'That' was the ice-cream van.

'We'll never get all these in there.'

'Bet you,' said Guy, and tried.

Karen watched him struggling. 'You're mad you, d'you know that?'

Guy balanced a chair on his head. 'I know, only I thought you wouldn't notice.'

'But I love you for it,' she said.

They parked the van outside the house and went to collect their keys. The landlord opened the door a crack and poked his head round.

'It's you, is it?'

'Yes. Your new tenants.'

'Sorry lad. I've changed me mind. It's gone to someone else.'

'That's not fair,' protested Guy. 'You agreed yesterday.'

'Students, aren't you?'

'What of it?'

'I don't let to students.'

'Why not?'

'And you're not married.'

'So?'

'I keep a decent house.'

'For goodness sake, this is the nineteen eighties.'

198

But the landlord was adamant. They trailed back to the van, very disappointed indeed.

The van was on the same street corner as it had been the previous day, and the children who had been their customers had seen it there. By the time they got back there was a crowd of people waiting with money at the ready.

'At least we can do something,' said Guy. 'Business looks good.'

'How can we sell anything?' said Karen. 'We can't get at the freezers.'

'I'll soon see to that.' Guy untied the back doors of the van and started to unload the furniture. Willing hands took it off him.

Karen had an idea. She pointed to a place at the back of the pavement. 'Put it there,' she said. 'Table in the middle, chairs round.'

'What's that for?' asked Guy.

Karen climbed in the van and reached for the ice-cream scoop. 'Might as well use the chairs, even if we don't have a flat to put them in,' she said.

'Good idea,' said Guy. He waved some of the customers towards the chairs. 'Sit down,' he said. 'Make yourselves comfortable. Bring back pavement cafés to Wavertree.'

On the day that Gordon was due back from France, Annabelle cleaned the house feverishly. 'I don't know why you're doing that,' said Paul. 'Can't Carol do it? I thought that's what cleaners are for.'

'I want the house to be properly clean.'

'Why else do we employ Carol?'

'I want it special for Gordon. So he'll know he's welcome.' Annabelle looked at Paul, wondering how he really felt about seeing Gordon again.

'We got on all right when we went to see him in France,' he said.

'That was a holiday. These things are easier abroad, aren't they?'

Paul couldn't deny she was right. He looked for what reassurance he could. 'His letter was nice.'

'Yes. I just wish he'd been more specific about whether his friend is a boy or a girl.'

'We'll know soon enough, won't we?'

'At least it'll be all out in the open this time.'

'Whoever it is, if it's a boy, we'll have to put up with it. We mustn't show any disapproval.'

'You do disapprove though, don't you, Paul?'

Paul had to admit it. 'Yes. Something like that, it's not what I'd hoped. It'll take some getting used to.'

'Perhaps we won't have to.'

Gordon's friend, when they arrived, was introduced as Cecile, and she was, to Paul's huge relief, a woman. She seemed to be quite a lot older than Gordon, thirty to his eighteen, but definitely female and very charming indeed.

'It's very nice of you to have me,' she said. To Paul's further relief she spoke fluent English.

'Not at all. We're very pleased to see you,' said Annabelle. 'Very pleased indeed.'

Gordon showed Cecile round the house and pointed out the families in the Close. 'It doesn't look much changed,' he said.

'I wouldn't say that,' said Annabelle. 'There's a new family at number eight.'

'And a new husband for Heather.' The unspoken question that was never asked hung in the air: Have you changed?

There was, Annabelle decided, nothing to do but to try and find out from Cecile.

An opportunity came later in the day, when the conversation turned to Gordon's visit to his sister Lucy. 'They're staying in the South of France,' he said. 'A grotty apartment in the backstreets of Marseilles.'

'They?' asked Paul. 'Is she still with Barry Grant?'

'Yes.'

'And are they ... do they seem to intend to stay together?'

'I think so. They seem happy enough.' The look on Paul's face gave the game away. 'You do not like this Barry?' asked Cecile.

'No we do not,' agreed Paul.

'He seemed very nice when I met him.'

'You went with Gordon then, did you?' asked Annabelle.

'Yes. Lucy asked me. This is a very kind family.'

'That's nice.' Annabelle spoke with feeling. Surely it must mean something if Cecile had been invited to stay with Lucy. Perhaps it meant that she and Gordon were more than just friends.

Gordon shared some of his plans with his parents. 'I'm thinking I ought to get some qualifications in England. It is my country after all.'

'How are you going to do that?'

'Enrol at the local FE College. Catch up on my O and A levels.'

Paul was delighted. 'That's an excellent idea. It's a pity to waste your brains.'

'There's only one thing . . .' said Gordon. 'I'd need somewhere to live.'

Annabelle was quick. 'You'll live here, of course. It's your home.'

'You're sure you don't mind?'

'Of course we don't mind. We'd be delighted.' Annabelle looked at Cecile. Where did she fit into this? 'Will you be staying in England too?' she asked her.

'Yes. But not here.'

'You'd be very welcome.'

'That's kind. But I must work. I have a teaching job in Chester. I must go next week.'

Annabelle was pleased. 'Chester's not far, you can visit us often. And Gordon can visit you.'

'Yes. I would like that.'

Paul and Annabelle were feeling very much happier.

Cecile stayed behind when Gordon went to enrol at the FE College. Annabelle seized her chance.

'Have you known Gordon long?' she asked.

'A year at least.'

'That's good.'

'We like him very much, all the family.'

'I'm pleased to hear it.'

'That's why we were sad when he and Jean split up.'

'I beg your pardon?' said Paul. 'Who is Jean?'

'Do you not know? Jean is my brother. He and Gordon were so much in love.'

'Oh,' said Paul. 'That's nice.'

The words sounded ludicrous as soon as he'd said them; they were the opposite of how he felt. He didn't think it was at all nice that Gordon had been in love with Cecile's brother, quite the reverse. He'd been hoping, so much hoping, that Gordon would have grown out of his affection for young men. Now it seemed as if these hopes were dashed.

Annabelle needed to know more. 'Is that why Gordon's come home? Because he and Jean . . .'

Cecile took pity on her and supplied the words. 'Had broken with each other? Yes. He was so sad. I think he needed to come home to make a fresh start. I think it's wonderful the way you've just accepted him.'

Even with the good money Billy was earning at his new job, the Corkhills always seemed to be short of cash. Billy had never known anybody like Doreen for getting through money. Even the clothes party, which had been supposed to be an earner, turned out to have finished in the red by the time they'd paid for the wine. And Doreen had ended up buying several dresses for Tracy because she had looked so nice in them when she was modelling.

Billy decided that one way to economize would be to get rid of his car. He didn't need it any more now he'd got the car that came with his job and at least he'd save on the tax and insurance even if he didn't get much for it.

His idea was to sell it for scrap but Doreen thought otherwise. 'You can do better than that,' she said. 'There must be somebody round here'd give you a few quid for it.'

Billy was persuaded to give it a try, and stuck a notice on the windscreen offering the car for sale. He asked around at work but there were no takers. He tried Pat, but Pat explained it was all he and Terry could do to run their van. He did come up with an idea though.

'Don't park it round here, put it on the main road. That way there's more people'll see your notice. Put your address on, then they can come round if they're interested. After all, there's one born every minute.'

Billy tried it but it didn't result in a queue of willing buyers beating a path to his door. Quite the opposite in fact: there was still no interest.

Until Guy heard about the car. 'I might want it,' he said.

'You've got a car,' said Karen.

'Not a very good one. This might be better.'

'It's a lovely car,' said Billy. 'Come and look.'

Billy extolled the car's virtues as he and Guy walked up towards the main road. 'It's a smashing car. I'll be sorry to see it go really. But I have to use the garage for the firm's car, and it seems daft to leave it out getting rusty.'

Guy got into the car and turned the key in the ignition. Nothing happened.

'Of course, she can be a bit funny sometimes,' said Billy. 'You have to coax her.' He took Guy's place and played with the choke. It didn't help. He couldn't get the car to turn over either.

'Maybe something's loose,' said Billy. 'Let's look.'

Guy helped him lift the bonnet. They looked at the engine. Wires dangled loosely where the battery should have been. The battery itself had gone.

The car was a sitting target after that. By the time Billy came back with Pat, the van and a tow rope, the wheels had been lifted too. Billy gave up. In the end he had to pay to have the car taken away. What he got for the scrap value just about covered the bill.

*

Doreen, keen to foster the relationship between Ruth and Rod, had given Ruth a formal invitation to tea. She was going to do it right, just as she thought Ruth would expect. Little cakes, serviettes, sandwiches with the crust cut off. Even if the family did prefer egg and chips, Doreen was determined to show Ruth that she knew how things should be done.

Ruth decided to do her bit too. 'Come on,' she said to Rod. 'We'll go and get your mother a present.'

'What for?'

'Mothers like presents. Besides it'll be a bit of fun.'

'What we getting?'

'Don't know till we've got it, do we?'

Ruth took Rod round several shops, picking things up and commenting on them in a way that made Rod embarrassed. He wasn't used to girls like Ruth. She'd been brought up in an unconventional household and her response to that was to have learned not to care what other people thought. She was a revelation to Rod compared to his mother, who was always anxious about what the neighbours would think. But he wasn't altogether comfortable, especially on the visit to the flower shop.

Ruth dragged Rod in there by pretending she wanted some flowers for herself.

'What d'you want them for? You've never been keen on flowers before.'

'All girls like flowers, don't they?' Ruth said to the flower shop man.

'Well, what kind d'you want, then?'

'You choose whilst I look round. It's supposed to be a surprise, isn't it?'

When Rod emerged with a bunch of carnations, Ruth was standing outside with a pot plant.

'Where d'you get that?' he said.

'Where d'you think?'

'I didn't see you buy it.'

'Buy it? Who buys presents?'

'Then how?'

'I lifted it, didn't I? Picked it up and walked away.'
She moved as if to go back to the shop. 'D'you want me
to show you?'

Rod set off firmly in the opposite direction. 'I do not.
Let's get a long way away from there.'

'What's the matter with you? Scared or something?'

'It won't do me any good with me job, will it?'

'What do you mean?'

'I'm applying to join the police.'

Ruth's views about the police were the only thing she
had in common with Billy. The two of them had a lot of
fun at Rod's expense at Doreen's tea party. The fact that
it was only the two of them who laughed at their jokes
didn't stop them enjoying themselves.

'The policeman's ball,' said Ruth, 'is that a dance or a
raffle?'

'Why did they introduce compulsory safety belts?'
asked Billy.

'Why?'

'So you don't fall out the car when the police shoot
you.'

Doreen did her best to stop them. 'You were glad
enough of the police when you needed them,' she said to
Billy.

'When they're there,' said Billy. 'Were they there when
my car battery was stolen?'

'Probably waiting round the corner till it was safe to
have a go at the wheels,' said Ruth.

And she and Billy laughed again.

It was time for the start of the school term, and Nick
used this as the excuse for persuading Scott to go back to
his mother's. 'It's easier to get to school,' he said, 'and all
your things are there. Ginny can't get on your back too
much if you're out all day.'

In fact the real reason for shifting Scott was that

Heather was due back from her trip to Hong Kong. Nick wanted her to come back to peace and quiet.

He arranged to take the afternoon off to greet Heather, but he was held up and she got back before him. Someone else got there before him too. Charlie knocked at the door a few minutes after Heather had arrived home and was joining Heather with a cup of tea by the time Nick arrived.

Nick was not pleased. He'd very much wanted Heather to himself, and if he had to share her with anybody, Charlie was the last person he would have chosen. It didn't help that Charlie and Heather were getting on well.

'You didn't tell me Charlie had been to Hong Kong,' said Heather.

'Oh, he gets about.'

'The happy wanderer, that's me,' said Charlie.

'Has he been telling you tales?' asked Nick.

'He saw a different Hong Kong to me. I think if I'd heard some of this before I went I wouldn't have dared go.'

'Charlie likes embroidering things.'

'No point in going to a place if you don't see the local colour,' said Charlie.

'All I did was stay in this really dull hotel and meet these really boring accountants.'

'I'm glad to hear it,' said Nick.

'All they could talk about was money.'

'You don't know what you missed,' said Charlie.

'I didn't realize there was an altogether different life going on just under my nose.'

'It's amazing how much goes on under your nose,' said Charlie.

'I don't know how to put this,' said Nick, 'but Heather's had a long journey. Maybe she'll want a bath and some rest.'

'All right, I get the message.' Charlie got up. 'Nice to meet you, Heather. At last.'

'It's mutual. I began to think Nick'd never let us get to know each other.'

206

'There you are, Nick,' said Charlie. 'No harm done.'

'What did that mean?' said Heather, when Charlie had gone.

'Don't ask me. And does it matter? At least you're here now.'

Their reunion was as good as their honeymoon. 'You know something?' said Nick the next morning. 'I almost don't mind you being away if it's so nice when you get back.'

'I'll try not to go away again too soon. It's lovely to have the place to ourselves. Has Charlie been around much when I was away?'

'No. Why do you ask?'

'He seemed so much at home, that's all.'

'Don't let's talk about Charlie. Let's talk about us.'

Pat was far too enraptured by Andrea Parkin to be put off by Terry's warning. The only trouble was that he had to let Andrea make the running. She'd made it pretty plain that she'd phone him, and that she didn't want it the other way round.

However, true to her word, she arranged to come up to the Close to discuss putting some van hire business their way. Pat dressed carefully for the meeting.

'What's the funeral gear for?' asked Terry.

'This is my new shirt. I'm expecting a visitor.'

'I can guess who,' said Terry. 'If I'd known I'd've put my own funeral stuff on. 'Cos if Bernie Parkin finds out you'll be dead and buried.'

'It's business,' said Pat.

'Pull the other one.'

'Haven't you got work to go to?'

Unfortunately for Pat, the clean shirt and the empty house and the bottle of wine he'd bought were in vain. Andrea phoned, two hours late, to say she couldn't make it. Pat contemplated the bottle of wine. The only thing left was to drown his sorrows.

He got up late the next morning, feeling very far from his best, and came downstairs dressed only in a pair of boxer shorts and with a splitting head. Terry was unsympathetic. 'I told you she was a man-eater. She's just playing with you.'

'Give us a break. Put the kettle on.'

'Let's hope this teaches you a lesson. Didn't I tell you to leave her alone?'

Pat was in the kitchen making black coffee when there was a knock at the front door. Terry looked through the window to see who it was.

'Oh no.'

'What?'

'It's her.'

Pat rubbed his unwashed face. 'I can't let her see me like this.'

Terry thought quickly. 'Go out the back way. Then when I've let her in you can come in the front and go upstairs.'

'You're a pal, Terry. Thanks a lot. I knew you'd see I was right.'

Pat, in his boxer shorts, got round to the front door to find himself locked out.

Inside the house, Terry was entertaining Andrea. He was keeping her away from Pat for Pat's own good. 'Pat had to pop out.'

'On business?'

'Not exactly. He just wasn't expecting you this morning.'

Across the Close, Pat took refuge with Heather. She looked at his bare legs.

'Would you like to borrow a pair of trousers?' she said. 'I'm sure I've seen an odd pair lying around upstairs. You can't walk about like that.'

'I'd love you for ever. And would you mind if I just had a wash? And maybe borrowed Nick's comb?'

'Sounds like you haven't got a home of your own.'

'It feels like that too.'

'Is this Terry's idea of a joke or something?'

'Or something.'

So Pat met Andrea for the second time wearing a pair of borrowed trousers.

It was when he returned them that the trouble started. He gave them to Heather.

'Thanks a lot,' he said.

'Any time.'

'And this was in the pocket.' Pat produced Charlie's cheque book. 'Friend of yours is he? These must be his then.'

When Pat had gone Heather confronted Nick. 'What are a pair of Charlie's trousers doing in my house?'

'I'd better explain about that.'

Heather was cool. 'Go on.'

'Well, he stayed here.'

'How long? The whole three weeks?'

'One night, just one night, that's all.'

'Why didn't you tell me? I thought you said he hadn't been round much whilst I was away.'

'I suppose I forgot.'

Heather was angry. 'Nick, I don't believe you. For weeks now you've kept me and Charlie away from each other. When you got home and found him here with me, you gave him a look that could have curdled the milk. Something's going on, and I want to know what.'

'There's nothing going on.'

'So why did he stay? And why did you not want to tell me?'

'You don't have to know everything, do you?'

Heather was sad. 'What kind of marriage is this, Nick, if we can't trust each other?'

Chapter Fifteen

The first few days after Gordon's return home were very difficult for Paul. It was one thing to decide in theory when Gordon was on the other side of the Channel that he would accept him as he was. Doing it in practice was harder.

Paul had been brought up to believe in simple certainties: hard work is a virtue, and virtue is rewarded; laws were made to be kept; men are men and women are women. Several of these certainties had been challenged over the last few years. The first challenge had been the redundancy that had brought him into Brookside Close. He had worked hard, he'd done a good job, and yet he'd ended up on the scrap heap.

His certainty about law and order was less clear too, after the business with the crossing. He was not ashamed of his clash with the police over that; on the contrary, he was proud of it. Now he was facing the biggest test of all. Could he accept that his own son was a homosexual?

Paul felt very sad. He was having to give up hope of so much he had planned for Gordon, almost as if Gordon had died. He'd been so proud of his son, he'd looked forward to him growing up, bringing a nice girl home, getting married, having children. Now there would be none of that.

It didn't help that Gordon didn't seem to feel anything like the same discomfort. He seemed to accept that he was homosexual without making any attempt to fight it. He'd changed a lot during his time in France and some of the changes were very much for the better. He was no longer timid, he seemed now to know who he was and what he wanted.

Annabelle found it easier to come to terms with the new situation. A conversation with Cecile helped a lot. 'You're not the first people this has happened to,' said Cecile. 'My parents were destroyed when they first knew about my brother.'

'How long have they known?' asked Annabelle.

'Oh, for some time now.'

'So Gordon wasn't the first . . .'

'No. But you mustn't think from that that my brother didn't care for Gordon. The relationship didn't last for ever but that can be true for all of us, can it not?'

Annabelle thought of Lucy and had to agree. The comparison made Gordon seem more normal. If Jean had been a girl it wouldn't seem so dreadful for Gordon to have had an affair and then split up. But Jean wasn't a girl.

'Have your parents got used to it yet?'

'Mostly I think. Certainly they accept my brother. He doesn't live at home but he visits just like any son would, and they receive him as their son. But then, so do you with Gordon.'

'I suppose we do,' said Annabelle. Suddenly, instead of being ashamed, she felt proud. Perhaps they were doing what was right in accepting Gordon as he was. She began to feel a lot better about the whole situation.

Her new cheerfulness was quickly put to the test. Gordon went out one day looking particularly smart. It was clear he'd told Cecile where he was going, but he hadn't told his mother. Eventually Annabelle just had to ask.

'Is Gordon keeping something secret?'

'He's gone to see someone.'

'A friend?'

'He doesn't know yet. He's gone to find out.'

'Oh. I don't want to pry, but I wish Gordon would tell us what is going on.'

'I'm sure he will, when he knows himself. If he thinks you'll accept it.'

'We'll do our best.'

When Gordon came back, he was all smiles. 'Do you remember Christopher Duncan?' he said.

'The head boy at school?'

'Yes.'

Annabelle gritted her teeth to avoid saying, 'The one who started all this trouble.' She was very glad she'd kept silent when Gordon carried on. 'I went to see him this morning where he works. And I wondered if you'd like to meet him.'

Annabelle, remembering the conversation with Cecile, found it in herself to be generous. 'Of course,' she said. 'Why don't you invite him to tea?'

Unfortunately this was altogether too much for Paul. 'D'you mean to say we're having him here,' he said, 'and you've invited him?'

'We've always encouraged the children to bring their friends home.'

'Friends, yes, but this isn't quite the same, is it? Christopher Duncan is more than a friend.'

'We don't know that, do we? Anyway it's done now.'

'So we have to go through with this ridiculous tea party, do we? You're asking me to sit round a table making small talk with the man who seduced my son.'

'We have to, Paul, if we don't want to lose Gordon. You don't want that do you?'

Paul struggled between his love for Gordon and his distaste for what was happening. He remembered Gordon as a baby and as a small boy: he'd been so proud of him then. And now this. What Annabelle said was true; if he didn't accept Gordon now he'd lose him altogether.

Annabelle saw him struggling and seized her chance. 'You'll just have to accept it, Paul. We both will. We've got to get used to the fact that our son's gay.'

One person who couldn't accept it was Carol, the Collins' cleaner. She had been working for them for over a year now but this was the first time she'd met Gordon. It didn't take long for her to put two and two together.

'Excuse me, Mrs Collins,' she said, 'could I have a minute?'

'Yes, of course.'

'I want to tell you I won't be coming any more.'

'Oh, I'm sorry to hear that. Have you got another job?'

'It's not that.'

'Is it the money?'

'No it's not. It's your son.'

'Gordon?'

'Yes. You've not told me the truth, have you?'

'What are you talking about?' Annabelle knew but she didn't want to admit it.

'You let me go ahead, didn't you, and clean that toilet and the sink where he cleans his teeth and everything.'

Annabelle knew what she meant. 'Are you scared you'll catch something?' Carol nodded. 'AIDS?' Carol nodded again.

'You've not been straight with me,' she said. 'I've got a child to support. What would happen to her if anything happened to me?'

Annabelle was hurt. 'I don't want you to think that we knowingly let you put yourself in a dangerous situation. You see, we weren't really sure about Gordon.'

Paul came through from the lounge. He hadn't intended to join in but this was too much for him. 'There's no need to apologize for our son, Annabelle,' he said.

Annabelle couldn't believe it. She was half alarmed, half delighted, as he took Carol on.

'People like you are frightened of AIDS without knowing what you're frightened of,' said Paul. 'You can't get it from a sink, you get it if you're promiscuous. Hetero-sexuals as well as homosexuals.'

'But it's homosexuals more,' said Carol.

'What you're really objecting to,' said Paul, 'is that our

son is a homosexual, and you think that makes him funny. Well, our son is a perfectly nice bright young man; he's not a diseased pervert and he's not promiscuous. You can leave if you like but we shall stand by him.'

When Carol had gone, Paul and Annabelle had a drink to steady their nerves. 'Thank you, Paul,' said Annabelle.

'No need to thank me. If you can't support your own family, who can you support?'

'But you were saying things about Gordon . . .'

'That's different, isn't it? It's not to say anybody else can. Anyway what I said was true. Gordon isn't promiscuous. Why else would he still be sticking by Christopher Duncan?'

'Does that mean you'll be here when Christopher comes?'

'I think I'll have to be, won't I?'

Paul's new resolution didn't prevent the start of the tea party being difficult. Paul changed his neckscarf for a tie, and his tie back to a neckscarf before he settled on a style of dress that seemed to be suitable. 'Do I look casual enough?' he asked Annabelle.

'Casual. But not very relaxed.'

'Are you?'

'No.'

In fact, things went better than they had expected. Christopher was polite, and he and Gordon behaved in a way that any old friends would have behaved together. He took a flattering interest in Paul's success in getting a crossing in Dortmund Way and praised Annabelle's cake. It might only be the beginning of what Annabelle and Paul would have to come to terms with, but it was a good beginning.

Although Heather and Nick patched up their quarrel over Charlie, married life after that didn't go altogether smoothly. Heather was rapidly learning that you don't really get to know someone until you live with them. Some days she was welcomed home with flowers and wine by the warm and caring Nick she had married. But sometimes he came in late with vague excuses. Increasingly Heather found his forgetfulness irritating rather than endearing.

The children were a constant source of friction, particularly Scott. After a couple of weeks of living with his mother he came up to Brookside Close again in search of a home. Nick agreed with Heather that although Scott would always be welcome as a visitor, it really wasn't possible in the long term for the three of them to live together. They gave Scott tea and then Nick took him home.

But the next day Heather came home from work to find that Nick had changed his mind and agreed that Scott could move in. She drew Nick to one side.

'What's going on? I thought we agreed he couldn't stay?'

'Did we?'

'Oh, Nick, surely you remember.'

'Whatever you say.'

'Don't put it all on me. I don't want to be the heavy step-mother.'

'It's your house.'

'Our house. And I want it for us.'

'Tell him then.'

'You tell him, he's your son. You can't expect me to take the responsibility.'

'Whatever you say.'

It was Nick's relationship with Charlie that caused Heather the greatest anxiety. Charlie didn't often come up to the house, at least not when Heather was there, but it was fairly clear that he and Nick saw quite a lot of each other at the flat. Heather tried to talk to Nick about it, but it wasn't easy. Whenever she started, he changed the subject or charmed her with soft words, and because she didn't want to provoke another row she let him do it.

She turned to him for reassurance in bed but that didn't help. He was often restless, getting up in the middle of the night, so that when she reached for him, he wasn't there. And when he was, he often feigned sleep, too tired, he said, for making love. Heather cast about for explanations. Perhaps she was expecting too much, making too many demands. Perhaps Nick needed more time to adjust to a new way of life; maybe it had been a mistake for him to come and live with her. She wondered whether to suggest that they should sell the house and make a fresh start in a home of their own.

It was when Heather saw Christopher Duncan and Gordon Collins together that fear about the nature of the relationship between Charlie and Nick hit her. Perhaps Nick and Charlie were more than friends. She tried to dismiss the idea as nonsense but it wouldn't go away. It would explain so many of the things that were puzzling her.

She tackled Charlie about it. 'Have you ever been married?' she asked him.

'Not me, lady. I'm too careful for that.'

'Meaning Nick hasn't been careful?'

'Did I say that? Nick's a lucky fellow.'

'Because he's got it both ways you mean?'

Charlie caught on. 'Are we trying to talk about anything in particular?'

'I suppose we are.'

'Why don't you come out with it then?'

'Because it isn't easy.'

'Too late to stop now.'

'All right. It's about you and Nick. Your friendship, it bothers me.'

'Don't let it.'

'Don't let it? How can you say that? I'm Nick's wife aren't I? Even if I don't always feel like it.'

'And you think that's something to do with me?'

'Yes I do. I need to know, Charlie. Are you and Nick . . . are you more than friends? Are you gay?'

Charlie smiled and put his arm round Heather. 'Why would you think that?'

'It's fairly obvious, isn't it? What else are all the secrets about?'

'Not that, anyway,' said Charlie.

216

'Promise me, Charlie?'

'I promise you. We're old friends, remember. We have a bond much stronger than sex.'

All Heather's fear and frustration came to a head one day when she came home from work to find Ruth there, deep in conversation with her father. They stopped talking when she came in as they so often did, making Heather feel like an intruder in her own home.

'Have I interrupted something?' she asked icily.

'We were just talking,' said Ruth.

'Again.'

'She was just going,' said Nick, 'aren't you, Ruth?'

'Why?' asked Heather. 'In case I find out what's going on?'

'Nothing's going on,' said Nick.

This was too much for Heather. 'Don't tell me that. I'm not an absolute fool. D'you think I can't see what's in front of my eyes?'

'Can you?' said Ruth.

'I may not know what it is, but I know there's something. Something you know, something Charlie knows . . .'

'Leave Charlie out of this,' said Nick.

'Why? What's so special about him? Why should he be protected and not me? I'm the one that's your wife, not him. Or Ruth.'

'Be quiet, can't you,' said Ruth. 'Can't you see you're upsetting him? He can't stand this kind of thing. It's bad for him.'

Heather turned on Ruth. 'Bad for him? How about me? All I want is to know what's going on.'

'He should never have married you,' said Ruth. 'I knew he shouldn't.'

The words brought tears to Heather's eyes. She turned to Nick. 'That's not true is it? Tell me you don't think we've made a mistake.'

'Heather, I'm sorry. I never meant you to know,' he said.

'Know what? What is there to know?'

But Nick didn't wait to tell her. He ran for the door before either of them could stop him.

Nick didn't come back that night. Heather had a pretty good idea where he'd be and who he'd be with, but she made her mind up that she wasn't going to look. The next move was up to him. If he wanted their marriage to go on, he would have to prove it by coming back to her.

She spent the night doing some very hard thinking. For a start she needed to sort out her feelings about Nick. When she'd calmed down, she realized that she still loved Nick and she didn't want to lose him.

But she was also very clear that things couldn't go on like this. The only possible hope of making this marriage work was for Nick to share his secret with her. If he did that, they might have a chance: if he didn't, they had none. In the small hours of the morning, Heather had to face the fact that she seemed to have made a disaster of her personal life.

Early the next morning, Ruth called round. She was distressed and furious.

'Come with me,' she said.

'Why should I?'

'He needs you, that's why. Don't think I'd be here if it wasn't for that.'

'That's a joke. Surely you mean he needs Charlie. Or you.'

'I wish that was true. I wish he didn't need you. I wish he didn't love you. If he didn't, none of this would have happened.'

'What do you mean?'

'He was all right till you came along. He was coping. But now you've messed it up.'

'What is this?'

'Come to the flat. I'll show you.'

All Heather's resolve not to go to Nick weakened. If he needed her she'd have to go. She picked up her car keys and followed Ruth.

218

When they got to the flat Ruth pushed the door open. 'Where is he?' asked Heather.

'In here.' She led Heather into Nick's bedroom. He was lying on the bed with his eyes closed, with Charlie on the floor beside him.

'Look,' said Ruth.

'What's happened?' asked Heather.

'You still don't understand?'

'What am I supposed to understand?'

'Can't you see?' Ruth picked a syringe from the side of the bed. The awful truth began to dawn on Heather. She took Nick's hand and rubbed it frantically, hardly hearing what Ruth said. 'He's overdosed. Because of you. He had it under control till you came along.'

'What under control?' But the question was superfluous. The truth had already dawned on Heather. Now she knew what Ruth had always known. She knew why Nick had kept the flat on, where his money went, what his bond with Charlie was. She knew the secret he'd been trying to hide.

Her husband was on drugs.

Karen and Guy eventually found somewhere to live, just in time for the beginning of term. It wasn't exactly a flat, just a room in a big house, with a kitchen, bathroom and lounge shared with other students. But it was theirs.

'Now are you going to tell your mother?' said Guy, when they'd signed the agreement.

'I know you think I'm being soft.'

'Yes I do.'

'You don't understand.'

'I understand very well. When are you going to grow up, Karen?'

Karen was offended. 'I am grown-up. You should know.'

'In some ways, yes. But how can you be really grown-up if you can't leave home?'

'You know what happened to me mam.'

'It's not just her though, is it?'

'She'll miss me.'

'And you'll miss her. And your dad, and Claire.'

'That's natural.'

'Yes, it's natural. But living at home for ever isn't.'

'A lot of people do. Till they get married, anyway.'

'Not students. If you'd gone away to some other university you couldn't.'

'But I didn't go away did I?'

'Maybe you should have. University's not just about work you know. It's about other things. Going out, making friends, being independent. You don't know what it's really like to stand on your own feet until you've tried it. Believe me, you learn a lot about taking responsibility the first time you run out of bog roll on a Sunday.'

Karen laughed. 'Is that the sort of thing that's going to happen?'

'Very likely. But nice things too. You've no idea how nice it is to be free.'

'I'm free now, mostly. My mum and dad are pretty good.'

'Yes. But you still can't tell them you're going to live with me.' Karen was silent, and Guy pursued his advantage. 'That's exactly what I'm trying to say. You're still thinking all the time about what they approve of and what they don't.'

'I care about them.'

'I know you do. And if they care about you, they'll let you go. You've got to risk it, Karen.'

Karen waited until she'd got her mother on her own before she started. 'Mum, I've got something to tell you.'

'Oh yes?'

'You know Guy . . .'

'I should do. He's been up here for his tea often enough.'

'Yes, well, that's because he's been living in hall. The food's awful.'

'So it's cupboard-love brought him here. And there was me thinking it was something else.'

'What?'

'I've seen the way he looks at you.'

'That's what I wanted to talk about.'

'Oh yes?'

'Now he's moved out, he's got this flat . . .'

Sheila had an idea about what was coming. 'Go on.'

'And he wants me to share it.'

Sheila was silent, taking it in. She wasn't pleased, but she wasn't horrified either. She'd miss Karen a lot but she knew this moment had to come. And one of the things she'd learned over these past few months was not to interfere in other people's business.

'It's up to you, love,' she said. 'I hope you'll be happy.'